DATE DUE

DC.RI 1-88	
ROSSO 7/84	
VILLA 12/88	
2-13-90	
MAY 28 1993	
DEC 27 1994	
BRODART, INC.	Cat. No. 23-221

THE ROMAN SPRING OF MRS. STONE

Also by Tennessee Williams:

THE GLASS MENAGERIE
A STREETCAR NAMED DESIRE
TWENTY SEVEN WAGONS FULL OF COTTON

THE
ROMAN SPRING
OF
MRS. STONE

TENNESSEE
WILLIAMS

ISIS Large Print
Oxford New York

Copyright © 1950 Tennessee Williams

First published in Great Britain 1958
by John Lehmann Ltd.

Published in Large Print 1986 by
Clio Press Ltd, 55 St Thomas' Street, Oxford OX1 1JG
by arrangement with
Martin Secker & Warburg Ltd.
54 Poland Street, London W1V 3DF

Reprinted by permission of New Directions Publishing
Corporation

British Library Cataloguing in Publication Data

Williams, Tennessee
The Roman Spring of Mrs. Stone
I. Title
813'.54   PS3545.I5362

ISBN 1-85089-139-7

Phototypeset, printed and bound by
Unwin Brothers Limited, Old Woking, Surrey.

Cover designed by CGS Studios, Cheltenham.

CONTENTS

PART ONE

A COLD SUN

At five o'clock in the afternoon, which was late in March, the stainless blue of the sky over Rome had begun to pale and the blue transparency of the narrow streets had gathered a faint opacity of vapour. Domes of ancient churches, swelling above the angular roofs like the breasts of recumbent giant women, still bathed in gold light, and so did the very height of that immense cascade of stone stairs that descended from the Trinita di Monte to the Piazza di Spagna. All day that prodigally spreading fountain of stairs had collected the sun-crouching multitude of persons who had no regular or legitimate occupation, and gradually, as the sun lowered, this derelict horde had climbed higher, like refugees of a flood climbing into the hills as the floodwater mounted. Now what was left of them crowded upon the topmost steps to receive the sun's valediction. They took it with an air of reverence on their still faces and hands, for they were nearly all silent and nearly all motionless now. Their livelier members, such as the urchin vendors of false American cigarettes who found the Spanish stairs a convenient place to skip out of sight and reach when occasion demanded, and the more successful mendicants who had wads of filthy paper to count in private, were already abandoning the tiny piazza at the head of the stairs and drifting down streets that would eventually bear them to Via Veneto where the American tourists thronged at this hour.

Among the dissolving assembly on the Piazza Trinita di Monte was the stationary figure of a young man who seemed to be waiting to receive a signal of some kind from the upper windows or terrace of an ancient Palazzo that flanked the higher reaches of the Spanish stairs. His beauty was notable even in a province where the lack of it is more exceptional in a young man. It was the sort of beauty that is celebrated by the heroic male sculptors in the fountains of Rome. Two things disguised it a little, the dreadful poverty of his clothes and his stealth of manner. The only decent garment he wore was a black overcoat which was too small for his body. Its collar exposed a triangle of bare ivory flesh; no evidence of a shirt. The trouser-cuffs were coming to pieces. Naked feet showed through enormous gaps in his shoe leather. He seemed to want to escape the attention which his beauty invited, for whenever he caught a glance he turned aside from it. He kept his head lowered and his body hunched slightly forward. And yet he had an air of alertness. The tension of his figure suggested that he was continually upon the verge of raising his voice or an arm in some kind of urgent call or salutation. But he had been standing there for quite a long time now and no signal had yet been given and the moment had not come for the call or the salutation. His watchfulness and his tension remained unabated, and when presently two figures appeared upon the terrace, five stories above the level of the piazza, the degree of this attention was even heightened. The terrace of the Palazzo still caught the declining rays of the sun and would continue to catch them for perhaps fifteen minutes after the Spanish stairs had given them up till tomorrow. The figures upon the high terrace were those of two women wearing dark furs, and the collars of these fur coats were turned up about their faces so that from this distance below them they gave an impression of being two exotic giant birds that were commanding a precipice. The young man watched them as anxiously as if they were birds of a predatory nature, likely at any moment to swoop down upon him and gather him up in their talons. While he watched, and apparently waited for something, his mouth tightened with discomfort, and secretly, fearful of betraying a thing so shameful, his long cold fingers crept inside his black overcoat and pressed themselves against the warm, aching centre of his body where hunger was and had been for many days and nights past since he had descended from the shell of a town among the hills south of Rome, and he knew that he would almost certainly sleep with it again. While he knew this, he observed without

5

looking at the figure of an American tourist who had stopped a little space away from him, under the Egyptian obelisk whose cryptic pagan engravings the man was appearing to study. But the young man knew that the hand in the pocket was about to produce a package of cigarettes and that he would offer him one. If accepted, that offer would have a sequence of others, dispelling hunger and every other discomfort for days to come. Still without returning the stranger's glances, his eyes assessed the value of the camera hung by a leather strap from his shoulder and the gold band at his wrist and even the approximate size of his shirt and shoes. But when the American tourist did exactly as he had expected, he shook his head curtly and moved a few feet away and then resumed his steadfast gaze upon the height of the ancient palazzo: for when a man has an appointment with grandeur, he dares not stoop to comfort . . .

* * *

In Mrs. Stone there was a certain grandeur which had replaced her former beauty. The knowledge that her beauty was lost had come upon her recently and it was still occasionally forgotten. It could be forgotten, sometimes, in the silk-filtered dusk of her bedroom where the mirrors disclosed an image in cunningly soft focus. It could be forgotten some- times in the company of Italians who had never seen her as other than she now was and who have, moreover, the gift of a merciful kind of dissemblance. But Mrs. Stone had instinctively avoided contact with women she had known in America, whose eyes, if not their tongues, were inclined to uncomfortable candour. Her present companion on the terrace of her apartment was someone she had known intimately as a girl but seen little of since then. They had run across each other that morning in the banking department of American Express. For such encounters Mrs. Stone had a stock phrase of evasion. How wonderful to see you, but I am just on my way to the airport! The other party might or might not believe her, it didn't matter, the important thing was that it released her with the utmost expedition. This morning, however, the phrase had failed to come out. The other woman's manner was too overwhelmingly aggressive. She cut straight through Mrs. Stone's momentarily paralysed defences. Perhaps the surrender was partially voluntary, for it was true that Mrs. Stone had lately felt, and almost admitted to herself, the need of discussing certain things in her life with someone she had known well in the past. There are intervals when a life becomes clouded over by a sense of irreality, when definition is lost, when the rational will, or what passed for it before, has given up control, or the pretence of it. At such times there is a sense of drifting, if not of drowning, in a universe of turbulently rushing fluids or vapours. This was the condition that Mrs. Stone had lately been conscious of, and she thought it might solidify or at least clarify things a little if she could talk them over, however indirectly, with someone from her own country with whom she had once had a fairly close connection. So she had said to Meg Bishop, Yes, come over this afternoon to my apartment and we can talk. I have so much to tell you. But a little while later Mrs. Stone became frightened of the impending exposure. It was as though she had consented to undergo a possibly fatal operation and at the last moment had lost the courage to submit to it. Just before it was time for Meg Bishop to arrive at her apartment, Mrs. Stone had called up other people. She had filled the apartment with the new acquaintances that she used as a shield against the past. She had hoped there would be no occasion for confidential talk, but Meg Bishop was not so easily put off. She was determined to have the sort of talk that Mrs. Stone was now so anxious to avoid, and once more Mrs. Stone's defences proved inadequate before the frontal assault of the other.

Meg Bishop was a woman-journalist who had written a series of books under the basic title of *Meg Sees*, all dealing with cataclysmic events in the modern world and ranging historically from the civil war in Spain to the present guerrilla fighting in Greece. Ten years of association with brass hats and political bigwigs had effaced any lingering traits of effeminacy in her voice and manner. Unfortunately she did not choose to wear the tailored clothes that would be congruous with her booming, incisive voice and her alert, military bearing. The queenly

mink coat that she wore, the pearls and the taffeta
dinner gown underneath, gave her a rather shock-
ingly transvestite appearance, almost as though the
burly commander of a gunboat had presented himself in the disguise of a wealthy clubwoman. Certainly there was no softness in her of that kind of
which Mrs. Stone had felt a need. There was probing
vision and there was keen analysis, but those were
the very things that Mrs. Stone wished most to avoid
at this moment. She had tried to keep her American
guest occupied with the Italians, but no fusion took
place. Miss Bishop made it plain that she did not
like the look of these people, she confined her
greetings to a succession of barely audible grunts as
Mrs. Stone conducted her from one little group to
another, and Mrs. Stone became so confused that
she could not remember the names of her guests
and she got their titles mixed up, and by the time
she had staggered through the introductions, much
as she dreaded being alone with Meg Bishop, she
was too weak to resist the arm that propelled her
forcibly out upon the terrace where there was no
one to interrupt a talk between them.

Soon as she stepped outside Mrs. Stone pretended
to find the air uncomfortably chilly but Miss Bishop
countered that strategy by insisting that both of
them put on their coats. I have got to talk to you,
she insisted, and that's impossible inside. So they
got into their furs and came back out. Mrs Stone
turned her fur collar all the way up to her cheek-
bones, but out of that insufficiently flattering shadow

her frightened and ageing face had the look of an embattled hawk peering from the edge of a cliff in a storm. She found herself treating Meg Bishop as if she were a brand-new acquaintance. She put on her grand social manner and talked as fast as she could in a strained, artificial tone, pointing this way and that way at various points of the Roman panorama, nearly all of which was visible from the roof of the Palazzo. But Miss Bishop responded with sceptical grunts as if she doubted every word that Mrs. Stone was saying. All at once she grabbed hold of Mrs. Stone's hand as it was pointing towards one of the seven hills of Rome and she said to her, Now let's stop this! At the same time she slipped an arm about Mrs. Stone's waist. The pressure of that arm awoke in Mrs. Stone a distasteful memory of the long ago girlhood when they had sometimes shared a bed in the dormitory of an eastern college. On chilly nights they had embraced for warmth, and then one time there had been a slight, abortive episode which had betrayed the possibility of a less innocent element in their intimacy. It was a thing so awkward, and afterwards so embarrassing, that perhaps it explained why Mrs. Stone had never afterwards felt quite at ease in the company of this old friend, though whenever they met she had felt obliged to treat her with the warmest display of cordiality and to speak and think of her always as "my oldest and dearest friend".

Do you hear what I am saying? cried Meg.

Mrs. Stone nodded although actually she had not

been listening. She had been looking through the glass doors at a young couple dancing in an almost stationary position and with no space between their bodies. They were now aware of her look. They separated self-consciously and Mrs. Stone made a sign to the young man. He appeared to ignore it. He lit the girl's cigarette and they turned their backs to the doors.

Nobody knows why you did it! Meg was saying.

Did what?

Quit the stage!

I'd had enough of it.

You can retire from business but you can't retire from an art.

You can, said Mrs. Stone, when you finally discover that you had no talent for it.

Talent, said Meg. What's talent but the ability to get away with something? And you got away with some effective performances in some very difficult parts. Of course it was a mistake for you to play Juliet at the age of Mrs. Alving. *Ho-ho! That* was an error! All that white satin and pearls were supposed to create an atmosphere of virginity but the illusion didn't work. When the violins played and that precious little Romeo came slithering under your balcony, I felt like shouting to him, Watch out, little bird, she'll snatch you up in her claws and tear you to pieces!

You mean I looked like a vulture?

No, an Imperial eagle!

Perhaps, said Mrs. Stone, that accounts for my failure in the part . . .

At that moment the young man who had been dancing behind the glass doors came out upon the terrace in response to another more urgent signal from Mrs. Stone, but he only remained a moment. He met the disappearing sun with a comic grimace of disgust and turned immediately back to the glass doors.

Mrs. Stone called his name, which was Paolo, and made a quick move towards him. But he didn't return.

I hate a cold sun, he declared, I don't like it when the heat's gone.

This remark of the young man made an unhappy impression on Mrs. Stone which did not escape the attention of the woman grasping her arm.

Isn't it odd, said Meg, how women of our age begin all at once to look for beauty in our male partners? You married and apparently were fond of a plump little man that looked like an Easter bunny. Why, I remember somebody saying, at the time, that Karen Stone must have married in order to avoid copulation! But now —

I loved Tom Stone a great deal, said Mrs. Stone sharply.

Maybe so, but he had no right to drag you off the stage and then drop dead a month or two later and leave you nothing but his filthy millions to fall back on.

I have fallen back on a great deal more than that, said Mrs. Stone.

For instance, what?

This country, these people . . .

If you mean that bunch of stately witches and epicene dandies that you've collected in there, why, all I can do is politely laugh in your face! They have a sort of elegance, yes, and the young ones are pretty and I have been told they make love very nicely. But is that enough to ask of a human society?

I think it is, said Mrs. Stone.

Escapism! said Meg. This was a favourite word of hers, it was a term of indictment she hurled against every aspect of the world of moral and intellectual weaklings that she felt herself appointed to chastise. Slowly under her eyes, like a morbid culture under the lens of a microscope, the phenomenon of Mrs. Stone had begun to assume the clarity and meaning of a symbol. She saw her not as an individual woman of leisure and wealth who had formerly been an actress but had abandoned the stage, presumably because of her failure in a part that was too young for her, but as the basic principle of a society and an age which had wandered through blindness into decay. She felt no pity. Pity she regarded as a mist upon the lens of analysis, and on this Roman terrace it pleased her to feel that she was conducting a miniature prosecution of the evil that was latent in all modern history, for the crumbling golden antiquity of the city beneath her and the ageing and frightened face of the woman beside her spelt the same abominable word to Miss Bishop, and that word was corruption.

I don't believe you're sincere, she was saying, but even if you are, and even if you did have more energy than talent, what do you think you are going to do with that energy now? Slip it in your pocket like the key to a house where you don't live any more? Energy can't be put into anything but action, and by action I don't mean sexual promiscuity! Yes, I am going to call a spade what it is! And you're going to listen to me. You took your typhoid shots before they let you step on the Queen Mary, and, by God, you are now going to take a simple injection of the truth from someone who cares enough for you to deliver it to you! I am shocked at you, Karen, I am shocked and revolted at what you seem to be doing with yourself, and I am not the only person who is! If you think that you have escaped observation here or avoided comment, why, let me relieve you of that misapprehension! There's been a fantastic kind and amount of talk, sniggering hints in every gossip column in New York and London and Paris! You can't escape from public attention any more than you can shake off the skin of your body. Let me tell you, the stock character of a middle-aged woman crazily infatuated with a pretty young boy, in fact with a succession of pretty young boys of the pimp or gigolo class, decorated but not concealed by some kind of phoney title, is —

Wait! cried out Mrs. Stone. She snatched at the encircling arm of Miss Bishop and tried to free

14

herself from it, but the arm only tightened and the voice went on:

No, you are going to hear me! I don't suppose you are going to pay any attention, but you are going to hear me! I came here to tell you just this. People know what you're doing. There isn't anybody who ever knew you, and certainly nobody who ever loved you, who —

Who are these people "who ever loved me"? cried Mrs. Stone. Can you mention some?

Thousands! You represented —

Various parts! But never *ever* myself!

Is this yourself?

What?

This female — *Tiberius!* — that you now seem to be playing . . .

The glass doors opened as if a wind had blown them from inside.

Mrs. Stone swept among her guests as if she were sweeping various garments aside in her search for a dress in a closet. When she arrived at the door to her bedroom someone touched her shoulder. Without looking back she struck at the restraining hand. Probably left it with the mark of her nails. And then the door was open, and then slammed shut, and the voices, the victrola music, the faraway clatter of the roulette wheel and the shuffle of dancers was no more, was in fact slightly less, than the sound of the faucet that flowed in the bathroom basin. She dashed the tepid water in her face. She made a gasping sound, but all of these expressions

15

of violent feeling seemed to have no association with anything that happened in her head. Her head was remarkably quiet as if a savage bird had been locked in it which had now flown out through some invisible opening. No. It was not necessary to take the sedative which she had thoughtlessly reached for. She set it down in the cabinet and closed the door which became her face in a mirror, and she saw the face looking at her, somewhat curiously, somewhat uneasily, and as she looked at it, a flush spread over the face as if she had surprised it in doing something that it was ashamed of . . .

The drift!

Going into a room and drifting out of a room because there was no real purpose in going in, nor any more purpose in going back out again. *That* was the *drift*. The drift was everything that you did without having a reason. But where was a reason for anything at all? Oh, you could invent a reason, and some were plausible. Some were plausible enough for being accepted the way a polite excuse is accepted for convenience or social policy. But there had been nothing. For a long, long time there seemed to have been that nothingness which had started when the pearls broke from their string and she clawed at a hand that tried to restrain her and then rushed out to resume the act of destruction on the stage that was flooded with very thin blue light like a wrapping of tissue paper through which she clawed with the talons of a chained bird. A long time ago. Sufficient not to remember. And what

16

was his name, the plump little man who lived with her? Deeply loved in some way that she could no longer remember. And all of that time, what was it? It had no connection with anything now existing. Or *he.* Or *it.* It was all a thing that had ended in a trick of some kind, some kind of stage magic by which it continued in spite of having stopped. Yes, stopped. Stopped. A word that imitated an end of action. Something thrown at a wall and arrested with a wet sound, and then dropped there. But she was not stopped, for she continued to drift. She had a glass in her hand, a glass of tepid water, which she was sipping, but she was not stopped there. She was going on drifting, now out of the bathroom, now into the bedroom, now out of the bedroom and out upon the terrace. And looking down, now. The light had disappeared. It was prima sera. All blue tissue-paper. But still down there, underneath the needle of stone that came from ancient Egypt, was the young man of remarkable beauty who had, yesterday, made an obscene sign to her. Down there, waiting . . .

She turned her back to him, shuddering with a disgust . . .

There was no sound. Everybody had left. There was nothing to do but drift about the emptiness of the rooms.

★   ★   ★

God pity you, said Miss Bishop as Mrs. Stone ran

from her, through the open glass doors, towards her bedroom. She did not pursue her, she let her go, for she had accomplished what she had set out to do, she had driven something sharp into Mrs. Stone's body. It was a reprisal for something a long time ago, and she was satisfied with it. But she felt shaken. She felt profoundly shaken. For some reason which was obscure to herself, she felt almost as unnerved by the prosecution as Mrs. Stone had been. That great clarity of mind on which she prided herself was momentarily disturbed and clouded, as if an aquatic monster had risen from the depths of an opaque sea without quite breaking the surface except by the surface stir of his movement beneath it. She shied away from it. She was not as analytical as she supposed. She was not as brave as she thought, and her understanding was limited to the huge alphabet blocks of collective impulse which she thought was the meaning of what she called life for the lack of a longer and more impressive word for it. In her state of disturbance, she turned the corner of the terrace and found herself standing outside another pair of glass doors. Through them she saw Mrs. Stone come into a bedroom. She saw her slam a door shut and lock it and fling her fur wrap to the floor and rush into a bathroom. Miss Bishop touched the handle of the glass doors but they wouldn't open, they were locked inside. She banged and rattled the door but received no answer. Faintly she heard the sound of a running faucet. So after a while she went back around the corner of the terrace,

18

thinking perhaps she would stay till the party broke up, but remain where she was, outside, by the balustrade of the terrace. She looked down from it, absently, into the well of the little piazza below. The last remnant of sunlight was touching the pagan inscriptions upon the dull rose granite of the obelisk, and directly beneath it, with his back to it, as if he were about to deliver a lecture upon it, stood the figure of a solitary young man of remarkable beauty. He seemed to be looking directly up into her face, in fact he seemed at the point of crying out to her or raising an arm in salutation. But Miss Bishop only glanced at him for a second. She paid him no real attention until a few moments later when she suddenly noticed that he had moved away from the obelisk and was now standing directly under the section of balustrade on which she was leaning. As his hands came out of his pockets and converged in front of him, she realized that he was about to make water against the wall. With a faint shock of revulsion, she drew back from the balustrade and returned to the interior of the apartment. The party was now breaking up. The music had stopped. The collection of "stately witches and epicene dandies" was drifting volubly towards the baroque vestibule where an elevator, that looked like the red damask box of an opera house, was waiting to remove them. No one looked at Meg Bishop while she glanced feverishly around to discover Mrs. Stone. But Mrs. Stone was nowhere

19

visible. She had remained in seclusion while the party broke up.

Still Miss Bishop lingered. The elevator was loaded and it descended. The remaining guests clustered in the vestibule waiting for it to return. Miss Bishop was still in the sala. She drifted over to the mantel, her attention caught by a French clock in a glass case. Under the case there was protruding a slip of magenta paper which Miss Bishop absently drew forth. She discovered that it enclosed a small photograph. It was the photograph of a blonde woman of indeterminable age with a face of unreal, mask-like beauty, and when she turned it over Miss Bishop saw written on it a very short message: "This is how I look now!" A mysterious statement, but possibly on the note-paper there would be something to explain its meaning. She picked it up, the slip of magenta paper, but just at that moment somebody touched her elbow. *What? Oh, yes, the lift!* — So she had to leave it . . .

* * *

Every afternoon about five-thirty Paolo went to a certain Parruchiere per Uomo e Signora on the upper reaches of Via Veneto. His barber was a young man named Renato who was no older than Paolo and almost equally handsome and only a shade less elegant. Perhaps Paolo didn't know it but this was really the happiest time of his day, the time, sometimes more than an hour, that he spent relaxed in the barber chair under the soothing, ruminative fingers of Renato. The sensuality of that hour was exquisite as the jam of the gods. The fingers of Renato were long and cool and as clean as water pouring from a silver tap. His eyes were dark and vague as Paolo's were, and his voice was caressing. Each afternoon's conversation was a sequel to the one before, beginning effortlessly where the other had effortlessly left off, and it was almost always about their women. Paolo was Renato's idol of elegance and fashion. Paolo, who was a bad Catholic, did not go to confession but went to Renato for a similar purpose, to give a spine of significance to his butterfly existence. Sometimes the long, cool fingers of Renato would linger for several minutes, quite motionless, on the delicate cheeks of Paolo while under them the patron's tongue and jaw-bones worked slightly and easily with his lazy speech. Indolence and sensuality flowed between the two of them like the commingling of two clear, tranquil streams under a shadow of willows. The chair was always turned at such an angle that both could watch the fashionable parade of the sidewalk at that hour when Romans go for their passeggiata. It was an agreeable habit, the late afternoon passeggiata, that Americans easily fell into, so that from the barbershop one could see, at that hour, practically everyone that counted in Paolo's world of wealth and elegant delinquency. One could see them through the windows and through the doorway that was curtained with deli-

21

cate, very pliable chains of dull silver metal that rattled musically when passed through. These metal links took the place of the glass door that was there in winter. Winter was well past now. The light metal curtain let the air in, now that it was ripening into heat, almost of summer, and also snatches of conversation from the sidewalk. Visual diversion was continual, so much that sometimes the lazy eyelids fluttered closed against it, the way that a hand hesitates in the middle of an excessively voluptuous caress, fearful of going on lest a climax of pleasure come too quickly.

Now that it was growing so warm the ministrations of the long, cool fingers of Renato were continually more pleasurable to his favourite young patron. It began with a shave, but continued with a massage that alternated luxuriously between the application of hot towels and mentholated cold creams. Paolo's young skin was flawless. It was the colour of very rich creams and almost as fine to the touch. The massage was pointless from a cosmetic point of view, but the luxury of it was the tacit excuse, as well as the talk, which the continual touch of face and fingers made so naturally intimate. While he was being shaved and massaged, Paolo, who was quite tall for a Southern Italian, sat far down in the chair with his legs dropping wide apart and with one hand laid on the centre of his being, which was his groin. That hand laid there was like an electric wire plugged into a socket for the purpose of giving power and light to the invariable subject of discussion which was the sexual experience by which and for which the young Conte Paolo existed. The indolence and luxury and dream of this connection between the two young men had been in effect for almost a year, during which period Paolo had recited the serialized history of three consecutive "protectors", beginning with the Signora Coogan last summer and almost at the same time, the fabulously wealthy Jewish Baron Waldheim whom they called the Baroness and talked of exactly as if he were a woman, and the brief but very brilliant association with the fashionable American lady, Mrs. Jamison Walker (whose husband had given him a black eye in Tangiers, but not before the lady had presented him with a pair of ruby cuff links from which he had realized two thousand five hundred dollars), and now, and for several months' duration, Mrs. Stone, from whom he expected to get a great deal more than from all the others put together, since she was the wealthiest of the lot and the only one whose interest in him appeared to be rooted in something deeper than concupiscence.

Paolo was too much the vain young dandy of the world to see or want to see much beneath the surface of a nature more complex than his. He looked at a person once, at their time of first meeting, and after that he remembered how they looked well enough to obviate another inspection. It was part of his coquetry as well as his enormous indifference to everything not himself to keep his eyes away from a person's face except for the languid and nearly sightless glances needed to point a question or a request. And yet even Paolo, with his minimal perception, had noted in Mrs. Stone the existence of a certain loneliness, unusual in kind as well as in degree, which a young adventurer no more encumbered by scruples than himself could turn to his great advantage once he got past her little wall of proprieties and defences. The defences of Mrs. Stone were somewhat formidable. She had been twice as long in the world as Paolo and had known in her profession a fair quantity of young men with languid graces and a measure of beauty who only looked at mirrors. They had not interested her in the past, but she had known them. She had liked them to play opposite her on the stage for they had so little resistance. It was like sticking your finger into a puff of meringue to take their measure, and yet they did well enough as supporting players. They felt and provoked no excitement. You knew what they were going to do and could obliterate them with a gesture. It was rather fun doing it. Sometimes it was nice to catch hold of their moist young palms in the wings and say, Don't be nervous! Every play has to open and some have to close ... Their dressing-rooms smelled nice, their bodies not giving off the musk of the male, or not enough of it to be detectable through the talcum or pine cologne. She had felt for them the sort of affection that is based on knowing you have the power to destroy and which is the warmer for being mixed with contempt.

24

It was only at first that Mrs. Stone had been able to identify Paolo with those young men whom she had dominated so easily in her professional past. Certain differences had soon become apparent. Somehow his petulance and languor did not make him girlish. Through the scent of his lotions of spice and rose was still detectable the musk of his gender, a thing that Mrs. Stone had always said she did not like about very young men and to which she was peculiarly sensitive. She observed it the first time that she met Paolo and told herself that it was unpleasant, and yet sometimes, lately, she would find herself standing near him only to catch it, remaining beside him after her cigarette was lighted or after she had placed a drink in his hand, staying there as though she were momentarily bemused over something. His hands were especially disturbing. On the table above the sofa in the library was a luminous globe of the world. It had an electric bulb in it. And frequently the hands of Paolo, resting on his serge-suited thighs as though infatuated by the feel of his own body, would appear as large and glowing as the two hemispheres of this lighted globe and she would fancy them placed upon her breasts, each of them covering each of her breasts completely and giving them warmth . . .

But Mrs. Stone did not let down her defences. These disturbing discoveries had only made her more watchful and uneasy. She told him good night at the door when he brought her home late, always becoming a little constrained in their last few minutes together, sometimes even omitting to offer her hand. Mrs. Stone knew, as well as Paolo knew it, that to become the aggressor in a relationship is to forsake an advantage. She, too, had once held the trump card of beauty which he was now holding and she had held it for such a long time that, although she now admitted to herself in private moments of candour that it was no longer hers, her social manner and procedure were still based upon its possession. She showed as plainly as Paolo that she was more used to receive than to offer courtship.

The afternoon of their first meeting, when the Contessa had brought Paolo to Mrs. Stone's apartment, he had left his engraved and crested card beneath an ash-tray on her mantel. The card had his telephone number in one corner and his address in the other. But days went by, and Mrs. Stone did not call him nor did she mention him to the Contessa whom she was seeing continually at that time. At last the Contessa admitted that the usual strategy had failed and that he had better make the first step himself. This woman is still very proud, said the Contessa, she has not yet reconciled herself to her age. She sat beside Paolo to prompt him with whispers and gestures the first time he called Mrs. Stone. The call was not satisfactory. Mrs. Stone was friendly, she was gracious and poised. She knew his name at once. She even mentioned the card left on the mantel. But she did not offer the invitation to cocktails or dinner that Paolo and his advisor had expected. It was necessary for Paolo to offer the invitation. He had to ask her to dinner and pay for the dinner himself. Mrs. Stone did not disguise her pleasure in his company but she continued to leave the initiative in his hands. It was not until lately that she had made the concession of telephoning Paolo. This was the only active move she had made and it was not enough to give him an upper hand. Paolo had falsely implied to his friends on Via Veneto that Mrs. Stone was his mistress. It was true that he had seen desire in her eyes, but that was where it remained, as in a mirror or behind a window. It did not spring out in response to his subtle enticements. Consequently his enticements had to become less subtle. His odalisque poses and languors did not turn the trick, and so one evening Paolo reached out and seized her jewelled fingers and placed them over his knee. He pressed the fingers tightly under his hand and then less tightly, but they remained where he had placed them for only a minute or two. Then she drew her hand gently out of his grasp and returned it to her own lap without being visibly shaken by the occurrence.

To Paolo it was a perplexing situation which was becoming almost untenable, for Paolo lived upon the current of time and it moved against him. The liquidation of the ruby cuff links, bestowed in Marrakesh by Mrs. Jamison Walker, had carried him brilliantly through a single season. But that season had expired. Something of the same nature, another access of fortune, had to occur very soon if Paolo were to avoid the step of retreat, of major concession, that leads so often to the entire abandonment of a campaign.

I *know* that she wants me, cried Paolo to the Contessa. Why doesn't she *say* or *do* something?

Patience, said the Contessa. Rome was not built in a day!

I am a Roman, said Paolo, but I am not Rome. If she doesn't make a move soon, I will have to start hanging out at the Galleria!

Do that, warned the Contessa, and we will be finished. The Galleria has an odour about it that gets not only in the clothes but on the skin and the breath! Even if you go hungry as often as I do, you have to be strong enough to play for all or nothing . . .

This was the state in which things stood one afternoon late in April when Paolo and his young barber Renato saw Mrs. Stone alighting from her Cadillac convertible, so close to their window that they could see clearly the slightly frightened, anxious look that her pale blue eyes always held when she was alone and thought herself unobserved.

My God, is *she* coming here? Paolo said in a startled whisper.

That lady? said Renato. She isn't one of our patrons.

Don't you know who she is? That, cried Paolo, is the Signora Stone!

Shrill whispers circulated the name about the shop. Towels cooled and lathered brushes dried as the entire company, patrons, barbers, manicurist and boy apprentice, fixed its attention on the lady hesitantly passing across the frame of the window. For those few moments something in her bearing, borne into exile from her time of greatness, held in suspension the mockery to which Paolo's gossip had exposed her.

I didn't know, said Renato almost apologetically, that she was such a great lady!

Paolo himself was impressed, not so much by the lady whom he alone knew, as by the impression that she had made on the others. It did not suit him, though, to hold a rock in his hand and not to throw it, and so the next moment he remarked to the company that she was not too great a lady to take a turn at the pump if a house was on fire.

Shouts of laughter demolished the moment of tribute, for the remark of Paolo was a play upon a certain idiom of the streets which had a specially bawdy connotation. To Paolo this was a gratifying reprisal for the position in which Mrs. Stone's reserve had placed him. As he made the implication, he vowed to himself that he would make it true. The reserve would crumble, it was already crumbling. Yesterday she had called him twice and the second time he had yawned on the phone and excused himself from keeping an appointment. Probably she was thinking about him now, even perhaps searching for him along the boulevard. Her dyed blonde hair, he could already feel it straining against the pull of his fingers and her hot breath, wanting

29

his mouth, forced downward while he would squirm in simulated transport. That could be done, yes, he would bet his life on it and he would do it! In spite of her skill as an actress, the violet eyes of Mrs. Stone betrayed her. There was a rapacious bird in them that he could release from confinement, and not to the clouds...

As though she had heard the laughter in the shop and known herself the cause of it, Mrs. Stone raised a gloved hand to shield her face and began to move in a direction opposite to the one in which she had first started, threading among a cluster of sidewalk tables before an adjoining restaurant in the manner of someone making an anxious search. She had not yet disappeared from the window-frame when she acquired a follower. A certain young man who had loitered upon the corner for more than an hour turned up his coat collar to conceal the absence of a shirt and started moving at a discreetly calculated distance behind her. Renato laughed at this and Paolo's feeling of triumph was dissipated. The young man taking after her reflected unfavourably, he felt, on his own association with Mrs. Stone. He sat up straight and drew his knees together, severely cutting off the contact between his thigh and the laughing young barber's.

Subito, subito! he muttered. I have an appointment to keep.

★ ★ ★

Mrs. Stone felt confused in the dazzle of light on the spring walks of Rome. All the glass windows were kept so highly polished that one could sometimes barely see behind them. Not knowing which way to turn, where to go she felt foolish. Strangers must think she'd been drinking. Being purposeless was like being drunk. In New York she had always had an appointment to keep, some place to be at a certain time: here, *never!* She was free to drift for hours in no particular direction. The only appointments she kept were with Paolo, and Paolo's appointments were always a bit indefinite. I will call you in the morning, he would say, or I will pick you up for cocktails. Rarely anything at a fixed point on the clock. Sometimes he failed to appear at all. This was one of those afternoons when she had not seen or heard from him, and it made her realize how completely her Roman life was hung upon this relationship, like the cloth of a tent that would collapse into loose folds without the central post that supported it.

Now she opened her handbag and fished among its contents for her pair of sunglasses, but she didn't find them. It was extraordinary how many things she was forgetting these days. There was nothing much on her mind, really there was practically nothing on her mind except Paolo, and yet she was more preoccupied than she had ever been during the most anxious period of preparing for the opening of a new play. She stopped again on the sidewalk, right in the middle of it, so that pedestrians from both directions had to detour around her. She blinked vaguely at the shop windows and tugged a little at the wide brim of her hat. Moisture was coming into her eyes. If the glare made her cry, the black dye on her lashes would dissolve. So she hastily resumed her stroll and at the first corner, she turned off the main thoroughfare into a street that was relatively dim. The dimness comforted her a little but it did not remove her feeling of confusion. She really must stop somewhere and collect her wits. This was too idiotic! Why had she gotten out of the car and dismissed the driver? She could not even remember, now, where she had told him to meet her or at what hour. What was she doing, was she searching for Paolo along the streets, as a lost dog goes out sniffing after its absent owner? Surely it wasn't as bad as all that, and if it was even *almost* that bad, she had better sit down somewhere and try to think things out and come to some sane conclusion. A thing like this could drift into downright lunacy if it were permitted to get the ascendancy over one's reason.

She stopped again. This time she stopped in front of a long shop window and though she gave the appearance of looking in, she hadn't the slightest idea of what the window contained. She was only standing there to catch her nervous balance to orientate herself; but the moments lengthened and nothing happened in her mind. The contents of the window became a little more distinct. The window contained articles of finely tooled leather. Her eyes wandered indifferently among them, until she was startled by something. Someone was standing inside the dim shop looking out at her. The shop was closed, for this was during the long afternoon recess of Roman business, so that the interior of the shop was lighted only by the tree-shadowed light of the street. She could not see the man distinctly but he looked so like Paolo that she felt her heart give a little tug of excitement. An instant later she realized that the figure was not inside the shop. What she was seeing was the reflection of a figure standing at the other end of the long window but on the same side of it as herself. It was the figure of a young man, somewhat taller than Paolo, but of the same general type. She did not look at him. Afterwards she was not sure what had warned her not to. Something had. Something had warned her not to turn her eyes towards him, and so she hadn't. She had continued her pretence of inspecting the leather goods in the window, waiting nervously for the man to go on. But he also lingered there. When she heard the faint sibilance of running water, Mrs. Stone did not immediately associate it with what the other loiterer was doing. Rome is full of the sound of running water, near or distant, loud or barely distinguishable, running water and stone steps are almost as much the signature of the city as the cream-coloured domes against the blue sky: and it was not a thing easy to believe, that the man standing at the other end of the window would be urinating against it. It was not till the sound began

33

to diminish that it identified itself to her. Then she was so startled that she uttered a slight, audible cry. She turned instantly away from the window and started in the opposite direction down the walk, very hastily now, till she came to the entrance of a little hotel where she went inside to recover from the shock. In itself the incident was not really shocking. What shocked and troubled her was the fact that she realized that this was not the first time that this particular figure had made himself noticeable to her. Far more frequently than chance could account for, this same young man had placed himself in her path and solicited her attention as she went about the city, never in this shocking fashion before, but always as if he were trying to give her some kind of a secret signal . . .

* * *

Three events of great importance and impact had occurred within a year of each other in Mrs. Stone's life. They were the abandonment of her profession and her husband's death and that interval of a woman's life when the ovarian cycle is cut off. Each event had been a severe shock in itself, and the three together had given her the impression that she was now leading an almost posthumous exist-ence. She had selected Rome as being somehow the most comfortable place to lead that kind of existence, perhaps because so much of it seemed to exist in the past. At first she had stayed at the Hotel

Excelsior, but there she was harassed by too frequent meetings with acquaintances among the tide of American tourists and movie people that the years after the war had brought over. Someone was always charging across the lobby before she could put on her dark glasses and crying out to her a greeting that carried the unspoken shock of her changed appearance, the hair that she was allowing to grey and the face and figure that had retired as palpably from public existence as her name had withdrawn from the lighted fronts of theatres. To escape these encounters she had taken her present apartment which stood like the solitary eyrie of a bird above the roofs of the city. She had two servants and hardly more than that many acquaintances in the city, while slowly her body became reconciled to its new condition and herself to the three separations which had unnerved her. The feeling of shock wore gradually off, and one day she had the former blonde colour of her hair restored and arranged with a riding stable near the Villa Borghese to resume the practice of riding each morning in order to recover some of her bodily firmness. Not long afterwards she took out her address book and got in touch with an aged Contessa whom she and her husband had met on a visit to Italy before the war.

The Contessa's voice shook with excitement when she recognized the name spoken over the telephone. It was not the thought of Mrs. Stone's importance as a theatrical personality that so excited the aged Contessa, but the recollection of the late

Mr. Stone's great fortune which was now presumably in the hands of this American widow. So great was her excitement that she became quite breathless and had to set the phone down for several moments with the excuse that someone had just arrived at her door. She walked to the window and inhaled deeply several times before she could resume the telephone conversation with controlled voice and collected wits.

Her artificial but convincingly effusive warmth went straight to the lonely heart of Mrs. Stone. She instantly accepted the invitation to lunch that was instantly forthcoming, and in this way Mrs. Stone was elected to provisional membership in a curiously special province of Roman society.

That was more than two years ago.

Mrs. Stone's meeting with the boy, Paolo, was fairly recent and had also come about through the elderly Contessa. Paolo was not the first Roman youth that the Contessa had presented to her. There had been three others, and Mrs. Stone's association with each had been rather expensive to her in spite of the fact they had served her only as escorts. A more intimate form of service was probably what each of them was prepared to offer but Mrs. Stone had not required it of them. At the point where each of them had approached her, with slightly varying excuses, for the loan of a considerable sum of money, always with the intimation that this would place them more completely at her disposal, Mrs. Stone had drawn back. Not disdainfully but rather sadly she had made them the loans, assuring them, at the same time, that they had misunderstood her desire for companionship, and she had not seen them again. What Mrs. Stone did not know was that each of these solicitations had been prompted by the Contessa and that the sums secured had been divided with the old lady. This was at first unknown to her but she came to suspect it, for promptly after the dismissal of each young man the old lady would appear with another, much like a merchant displaying a series of articles to a customer hard to please. Mrs. Stone began to suspect this connivance. It disappointed and pained her, it even, perhaps, humiliated her slightly, but she did not stop seeing the old lady. The stately witch had a certain enduring gallantry that had to be respected despite her chicaneries. Mrs. Stone was not long in discovering that this social patroness of hers had descended through poverty and age into a very marginal area of the aristocratic and fashionable world in Rome, and Mrs. Stone was almost as quick to decide that this particular sphere was the one most convenient to a woman who no longer wanted to bother with pretension and effort of any kind. For she was now, Mrs. Stone, in that disenchanted but relatively insured position of knowing not only what it was, or might be, that she wanted but what she was most likely to have coming to her. Knowing does not need to be consciously knowing. There were few things about herself or the world that Mrs. Stone was determined to resist the knowing of. In the last year or two, the time since the death of her husband and the abandonment of her career, there had been a great but soundless and invisible collapse of barriers in her mind, a great entrance and blowing through of candid acknowledgements, but these did not have to be inscribed on the walls of her rooms. They could be known without even saying, I know them. The drift had direction, if it did not have purpose, and sometimes direction is all that we know of purpose . . .

The association between Mrs. Stone and young Paolo had not gone at all to the satisfaction of the Contessa. That lady decided that Paolo had undertaken to cheat her, for he had now been in almost continual attendance upon Mrs. Stone for three months without having secured anything more negotiable than some neckties and his dinners. When she visited the youth with her querulous importunities, he always put her off with one of her own proverbs, saying, Please be patient, Rome was not built in a day.

What the Contessa failed to understand, said Paolo, was that Mrs. Stone was no ordinary lady. She was a great lady, and a very great one indeed, and could not be treated as cynically, for instance, as old Mrs. Coogan had been treated last summer at Capri.

The Contessa was not at all impressed by these arguments. In the first place, she told him, there is no such thing as a great American lady. It is a contradiction in terms. Great ladies do not occur in a nation that is less than two hundred years old. And not only, she told him, was Mrs. Stone a social arriviste, but she had been an artistic mediocrity. Oh, yes, she had been a well-known figure, but the Contessa had been assured by persons who had seen her performances on the stage in New York and London that she was more of a personality than an artist. She had once been extraordinarily good looking, yes; one could still see remnants of that: she still carried herself on the street as though she were making an entrance upon the stage. Imposing she was and still handsome, but only a naïve boy who had had comparatively little contact with the great world would allow this façade to deceive him. Fundamentally, Mrs. Stone, said the Contessa, was nothing more than a harlot who had struck it rich and was now in a position to make disbursements where she had once received them, and like most women of that character and those circumstances her licence was peculiarly unlimited. There was no real dignity in her and no real pride, only the usual affectations of someone who has forced and purchased her way into prominence. This "great lady", said the Contessa finally, is in the process of becoming a "tipo cattivo". Her name is becoming a scandal. In a short while now, nobody will receive her in those places where I was foolish enough to present her, but that will not stop her. When Rome has been exhausted, she will move to Tangiers: a woman falling like that will never strike bottom!

I think, said Paolo, that you are being malicious. The woman is lonely and she is no longer young and she has retired from a very exciting career. But I am quite positive that her feeling for me is, yes, romantic, but not wolfish! She has made no move to get me into bed. She has never kissed me. We say good night at the door. And this is certainly a great contrast to what I went through with the Signora Coogan and the Baronessa Waldheim and even with the great Mrs. Jamison Walker. They were at me like wolves almost from the moment I met them, yes, they were a wolf pack and I had to take shots to revive me.

Faugh, said the Contessa, how you do lie! Everyone knows that you never gave in to the Signora Coogan. And the poor Baron, you drove him almost crazy although he swamped you with gifts. Mrs. Jamison Walker took you to Marrakesh where she presented you with a pair of ruby cuff links worth a king's ransom which you told me were glass! You know what I think? I think that you are infatuated with Mrs. Stone and I think that she is the only one of the lot that you have actually gone to bed with and are going to bed with regularly, all the time. Yes, I think you are lying about the whole thing, just lying and making excuses! While you feather your nest! And what about me? Last night I fainted from hunger. Yes, yes! Literally fainted from hunger, smelling the food as I walked in front of Rosati's! And I was with a group of Americans who give the street beggars enough to feed me all week! But did I admit I was hungry? Certainly not! I have pride, I asked for a glass of cognac and opened my purse as though to pay for it myself! While you dined with Mrs. Stone at the Quirinale! Stuffed yourself, you glutton! And you tell me you don't get anything from her, that I am malicious to think she's buying your . . .

Aspet', aspet' un momento! cried Paolo. You have the impression that I am a common marchetta?

Figlio mio! What else do you think you *could* be?

I am a de Leo! said Paolo.

And I, said the Contessa, was born into the Black World!

Davvero! said Paolo. And you will die in the Black Market!

The old lady gasped. She was not tall enough to strike him in the face as he leaned back from her so she doubled her fist and drove it into a part she could easily reach.

Paolo crouched on the sofa with histrionic groans.

Ecco! Ecco! the old lady gloated. I hope that will put you out of business tonight!

★   ★   ★

The next time the Contessa saw Mrs. Stone was at a suburban villa where both were luncheon guests of a Hollywood film producer making a picture in Rome. At this party she drew Mrs. Stone discreetly aside.

I understand, she said to Mrs. Stone, that you

have been seeing a great deal of young Paolo lately and as your oldest friend in Rome I think it is necessary that I should tell you a little bit more about him. You find him charming, don't you? Everyone does. He's the most charming boy in Rome, which makes it probable that he is also the most charming boy in the world. But there are certain things more important than charm.

What are these things? asked Mrs. Stone with unfeigned ignorance of them.

The true Roman qualities, said the Contessa, are lacking in Paolo! He comes of an impoverished but reasonably good family, although the title belongs to his uncle and was bestowed by the Pope about seventy-five years ago. There is one thing, however, that you must keep in mind about Paolo. Paolo is by way of being a little marchetta!

A what?

That is our word for a boy who has no work and no money but lives very well without them. How do you feel about such people?

Mrs. Stone could not help smiling noticeably at this question.

I have nothing against them, she said.

Good, good! said the old lady. As long as you know what to expect there's less danger for you. But make sure that you get your money's worth, cara! I think that the Signora Coogan was badly cheated.

The Signora Coogan?

Oh, didn't you know the Signora Coogan? She's

from America, too, and last summer she took Paolo
to Capri and they say that the Signora Coogan is
the only one in the party he didn't make love to,
and she was so nervous over it that the poor thing
broke out with a nervous eczema. She looked so
hideous with the rash that she flew straight to Africa
and disappeared in the jungles. However — there
is one nice thing about Paolo which is unusual in
a boy of his type ... I mean the kind that we speak
of as the marchettas. He doesn't have light fingers.
Not even the Signora Coogan could say that he
touched her jewels or anything else that she hadn't
presented him with, and you know the Signora
Coogan had some very important pieces in the way
of jewels. I have been told that she used to leave
them all night in a soap dish. Now in my opinion,
and probably in yours, too, any adult woman of the
world who will put one hundred and fifty thousand
dollars' worth of emeralds and diamonds in a soap
dish, not even in her private bathroom, behind a
locked door, but in a connecting bathroom between
her bedroom and another bedroom that opens on a
veranda — why, such a woman has no more right
to enjoy great wealth than a monkey, and the jungles
of Africa is where the Signora Coogan really
belongs!

For reasons which she could not immediately
fathom, Mrs. Stone found this anecdote of the
Signora Coogan and Paolo more disturbing than
funny. She looked across the room at the boy whom
the Contessa was discussing. He and the wife of the

film producer were dancing to a phonograph record and Mrs. Stone found herself thinking that surely such beauty was a world of its own whose anarchy had a sort of godly licence. She knew that she, too, had once had beauty like that and had enjoyed the anarchistic privileges of such beauty but that her licence to enjoy them had been revoked by the passage of time. She lived, now, in a world that was subject to worldly laws. Perhaps nothing as ignominious as the flight of Mrs. Coogan with nervous eczema into the wilds of Africa, perhaps nothing like that was in store for her, but certainly it would be foolish to hope that her tenderness for this dark boy and his extravagant beauty would terminate in anything that would add to her small store of comforts, now that her nights were spent beneath the moon of pause . . .

The Contessa had gone on talking for several moments before Mrs. Stone's attention returned to what she was saying.

What church do you belong to? the Contessa was inquiring with seeming irrelevance.

None, said Mrs. Stone. I was born a Methodist. Why?

Ah, said the Contessa. Then he will probably tell you the story of his friend and the wicked priest who operates on the black market!

What story is that? What for?

He will tell you how the wicked priest cheated his friend out of ten million lire on the black market, and he will try to touch your heart so deeply with this story that you will want to restore the friend's losses to him!

Oh, said Mrs. Stone, I don't imagine that I will be touched that deeply. I may be touched, but not for ten million lire! You see, Americans aren't so romantic as their motion pictures . . .

What a pity they aren't, said the Contessa sincerely.

★ ★ ★

A few hours later this same afternoon, which was now approaching evening, Mrs. Stone and Paolo were on the terrace of her apartment and Paolo showed evidence of falling into a very pensive mood, which he ascribed to a headache.

When Mrs. Stone touched his forehead, Paolo sighed. He threw one of his legs over the arm of the canvas swing on the terrace and lowered his shoulders to a reclining posture.

Would you like a negroni? she asked him.

No, I don't want to get drunk. If I do I will cry.

What about, Paolo?

A terrible thing has happened to a friend of mine.

Ah?

He has been speculating in the black market. I will tell you what he did. He was approached by this priest who is very high up in Vatican circles and this priest told him that he knew of a concern that had a huge lot of English and American army supplies that were left here after the occupation and which could be sold on the black market at a great

45

profit and he gave the priest ten million lire to buy up a lot of this stuff and the priest kept the money and my friend got nothing, and now it turns out that the priest took cocaine and had spent the ten million lire on cocaine and a woman. So Fabio, my friend, went to somebody else who was even higher up in the Vatican circles and he said, If you don't give me back my ten million lire that I gave to this crooked priest I will go to the Communist party and expose the whole thing and there will be a terrible scandal that will ruin the Demo-Cristiani in the election next spring. The Vatican was terrified, and they said, Don't go to the Communists, don't go to the Communists! They got down on their knees and pleaded, and my friend, who is very religious, promised that he wouldn't, and they said, Show us the receipt you got from this priest. So he gave them the receipt. And one of the important people disappeared with it and the others stayed in the room with Fabio and drank wine and prayed. And then finally they got him drunk, and he said, Where is my receipt and the money, and they said, but you don't *have* a receipt. *Where* is it, give it *back* to me! said Fabio. And they said, *What*, give *what*? We never *saw* any!

Paolo said all this in practically one breath, throwing his leg up and down on the arm of the canvas swing and twisting tormentedly about, heaving many great sighs and finally beginning actually to weep.

Mrs. Stone did not listen. She felt a great weariness and a great lack of interest as if she had heard the story a hundred times before. But the mention of ten million lire she did understand, and when the recital was finished, she had computed it roughly in dollars.

Paolo, she murmured, how soon does your friend need the money?

As soon as possible, or he will turn on the gas!

I am sure that he will not do anything as silly as that.

He is desperate. He writes poetry. His faith in the church is destroyed.

Paolo had gotten up and put on his jacket.

Ten million lire is a lot of money, said Mrs. Stone.

What is money when friendship is involved?

But when that much money is involved, said Mrs. Stone, I think it is usually more than friendship.

What is more than friendship! said Paolo. Friendship is the most beautiful thing in the world!

Who said that to you? Did Mrs. Coogan say that?

Mrs. Coogan?

Yes, but Paolo, I don't leave my emeralds and diamonds in a soap dish, Mrs. Stone said gently.

I don't understand what you are saying.

I have no emeralds and diamonds, just a diamond or two, but if I *did* have emeralds and diamonds, I'd never leave them overnight in a soap dish. And Paolo, another thing, caro! When the time comes that nobody can desire me for myself, I think I would rather not be desired at all.

She went inside from the terrace. It was the

moment before the lamps go on, when the atmosphere has that exciting blue clarity of the nocturnal scenes in old silent films, a colour of water that holds a few drops of ink.

In a few moments, now, if Paolo were going to leave her, she would hear the elevator door clang shut and the whirring motion of cables removing him from her. She waited anxiously for those sounds of departure but all she heard were the tiny cries of the rondini flittering past her window. Mrs Stone was relieved and she could not deny the reason to herself. She did not want him to go. And as it became apparent that he was not going, Mrs. Stone felt, for the first time in her life, desire not confused with any other impulse. She felt it quite divorced from reason and will. For it was not at all reasonable and she was entirely unwilling to feel desire for this boy who had just now discarded the mask of gallantry he had worn, the show of respect, to expose himself as what the Contessa had warned her, that afternoon, the boy really was. *Paolo is by way of being a little* — what was the word she had used? Oh, yes, *marchetta*! Something a little superior to a whore but still something on the market, superior mostly in being more expensive, an article of greater luxury and refinement, what the French called poule de luxe . . .

Mrs. Stone laughed harshly to herself, and the two sharp notes might have come from the attacking beak of a bird, as she recognized what had happened upon the terrace. The boy had drawn from his pocket a bill, marked payable in advance, for services to be rendered, and she had not made the payment, no, nor driven the bargainer off, but with a casuistry that was the equal of his had intimated — had she not? — that under suitable terms an agreement might be arrived at. *When that much money is involved I think it is usually more than friendship.* And had she not computed the sum in her mind, and was she not waiting, now, at this moment, for an adjustment of terms? With the other three youths she had behaved with dignity. She had paid for but not accepted their favours. However, the old Contessa had seen through her and with each rejection had produced a fresher and more enticing article on the counter, leading up to and terminating with Paolo. With Paolo Mrs. Stone had somehow permitted herself to enjoy the innocent notion that the fresher quality could mean a superior kind, one with whom an honest and dignified bond could be established. Well, now that extravagant myth no longer existed, the ugly thing was the true one, and she was alone. It was impossible, with dignity, to be anything but alone. And she was alone in this bedroom above the spacious Scala di Spagna. Only her eyes in the mirror had looked back at hers since she had come to stay here, and the bed was large and white as a landscape of snow that turned faintly blue in the dusk. Letto means bed, and a letto matrimoniale was what she slept in alone, the covers disordered only by her own turning.

And yet Mrs. Stone could not deny to herself

what she felt in her body, now, for the first time, under the moon of pause which should have given immunity to such feeling but seemed, instead, to have surrendered her to it. She felt incontinent longings, and while they repelled her, they gave her a sharply immediate sense of being. If the elevator had descended with the boy, Mrs. Stone would have slipped back into the desolate drift, the indiscriminate flooding, the undistinguished washing along and away of myriad objects in the current of time, jarring together one moment and then swept apart in a steady, formless welter, meaning less than a succession of images in a dream. This suspension was opposed to the drift. It was not like anything she had felt, one time or two in the past. The past was, of course, the time when her body was still a channel for those red tides that bear organic life forward. Those rhythmic tides had now withdrawn from her body, leaving it like a tideless estuary on which desire rested like the moon's image on a calm sheet of water. And all at once Mrs. Stone did not need to wonder why the difference was. The red tides had been full of danger because they had a purpose not part of her plan to hold an exalted position. What she felt, now, was desire without the old, implicit distraction of danger. Nothing could happen, now, but the desire and its possible gratification. Knowing this, she knew for the first time why she had married (as Meg Bishop said people said) to avoid copulation. It had been the secret dread in her, the unconsious will *not* to bear. That dread was now withdrawn. It had gone with the withdrawing tide of fertility and now there was only the motionless lake and the untroubled moon resting on it, passionless as the acceptance of a shrewd proposition on terms that suited both parties.

Mrs. Stone went into the bathroom and poured herself a tumbler of tepid water. Then she washed down a tablet of belladonna and refilled the glass and went back with it into the bedroom. She kept the glass in her hand. Her lips and throat were so dry that she took continual sips of the tepid water. She sat on the bed with her glass of water, taking little sips of it into her parched mouth and throat, while the air in the room turned darker as if more ink were released from a steady dropper. Her face in the mirror, which she could see at an angle from where she sat, became continually more indistinct and lovely, as the knowledge of having nothing to fear moved steadily deeper within her.

After a little while she stood up to remove her clothes and then she lay stretched out on the cool comforting surface of the white bed with the water glass resting within her reach on the table. All of this time there had been no sound of activity except her own quiet motions, but now she heard Paolo's footsteps across the terrace, and the opening of the terrace door and finally the steps coming directly to the door of her bedroom.

Don't come inside, I'm not dressed, she called out softly.

He walked deliberately in and seated himself

upon the edge of the bed. Evidently he had reconsidered his refusal of a drink for there was a bitter smell of campari on his breath as he leaned over. He did not lean all the way down to kiss her but only close enough to look directly and clearly into her eyes as he asked her this question.

Why did you want to know *when* my friend needed the money?

Because you are very young, said Mrs. Stone, and very foolish and very beautiful. And because I am not so very young any more and not so beautiful, but beginning to be *very* wise . . .

After a moment's reflection, Paolo nodded, barely visibly, and then he leaned all the way down with open lips; but already, before he had completed that gesture, her arms and her head had risen as if the moon on the water had turned to a bird that sprang skyward . . .

★ ★ ★

The winter and early spring had been to the entire satisfaction of foreign visitors to the city who had chosen gold weather in preference to the more febrile indoor distractions of the two great Northern capitals of Europe. The sky was perpetually stainless as the glass heaven of the ascending paraclete at Saint Peter's, and each day had gathered a degree more warmth than the day before. Those tiny swifts the Romans called rondini had now returned to the city. During the day they hovered invisibly high towards the sun but at dusk they lowered a quivering net to the height of Mrs. Stone's terrace. To Mrs. Stone the city itself appeared to be performing some leisurely trick of levitation. Each spring morning when she came out on her terrace, the intricately-woven and gold-dusted web of the streets in which the domed churches stood like weaving spiders, seemed to have lost more gravity, to be floating gradually, weightlessly upward into the blue-gold warmth of the days, all serenity, all buoyancy, and making no effort. Such a thing is possible only in a youthful condition which Mrs. Stone had now passed. Sometimes it lightened her heart to look down on it, but that was only momentarily, and the longer and more consistent effect was a feeling of apprehension, a feeling that something was about to turn out badly, which feeling was perhaps no more than the wearing off of that protective detachment she had worn during the year after her husband's death, a retreat which could not be healthily maintained any longer and from which she was now emerging into a more normal degree of sensibility. Whatever it was, it broke the stillness in her and made her increasingly fretful and anxious, was all the worse for being without any reason on which she could put her finger.

In the mornings, now, she could sun-bathe on her terrace, in a small roofless tent of white canvas. Her body turned golden, but the gold was not perfect. It contained tiny creases which would not disappear beneath the oily fingers of the masseuse who visited her daily; the excess tissue which had accumulated during the year of neglect had been melted away by exercise and rubbing, but these tinier signatures of time, the little creases, stayed on her, ineffaceably.

Sometimes Paolo would also undress in the small white tent and lie on a cot beside her. She could not bear to look at him. He was too lustrous. The sun leapt down the air towards him like a child towards a child, and she felt ignored and excluded, and usually she would reach down to cover herself, outcast, ashamed, in the company of such affinities as Paolo's nude flesh and the sun. One time she cried. She averted her face and covered it with her dyed hair while she wept beside him and he obliviously dozed with a faint, childish smile on his lips and a hand curved over his groin to protect it from burning.

One day they had a quarrel.

A cloud had come up and the terrace was briefly immersed in a chilling shadow and she had complained about it. Paolo had suddenly sat up and fixed her with a Roman frown.

You don't want it to rain?

Of course I don't, I hate it!

I don't suppose it has occurred to you that there are some other considerations beside the amusement of rich foreigners here. I don't suppose you think it matters that the grain in the country is drying up from lack of rain and that the water supply of the city has been so reduced that they are having to turn off the electric current for two days out of the week!

Oh, Paolo!

Oh, Paolo! he imitated her. Well, you rich American ladies are the new conquerors of Rome. At least you *think* that you are. But let me warn you, this town is three thousand years old, and all of its conquerors have gone back to the dust!

She waited a little while and then she said to him quietly:

Paolo, were you a Fascist?

I am an aristocrat, he told her.

Is that the answer?

Some were Monarchists, said Paolo, but they were old or stupid. When I was fifteen I was already a pilot and I was the leader of a flying club called the Doves and we had light blue uniforms with gold doves embroidered on the sleeves. I had command of 15 doves. Six of my doves were shot down in flames over Africa. They were my fortunate doves.

His hand flickered across his bare chest in a sign of reverence.

Mrs. Stone did not believe the story of the doves. It sounded like the heroic fantasy of a boy scout. Paolo's fancy was agile but often contradictory and only a week before he had told her a similar tale, only there had been tanks instead of planes and the uniforms had been scarlet and the name was Tigers, not Doves, and furthermore, when he took the wheel of her car she had discovered that he did not know the clutch from the brake nor the position of gears and had driven so erratically that her driver, displaced to the rear seat, had started praying out loud and muttering pazzo, which had so infuriated Paolo that he had demanded that Mrs. Stone discharge him on the spot and had sulked for half an hour afterwards because she had gently declined to do so.

Last year, Paolo was now saying, we discovered that one of my doves was loitering every night in the Galleria. A secret meeting was held at midnight in the wine cellar of an old castle. The corrupted dove was brought to trial and everyone spoke in Latin and wore black masks and held white candles and the verdict was delivered in Latin and after the verdict a young priest, who was also one of my doves, heard the bad dove's confession and gave him absolution and then he was offered his choice of a pistol or poisoned wine or a leap from the tower of the castle.

Poor boy, said Mrs. Stone gently. Which did he choose?

He took the leap, said Paolo.

And Paolo was now so engrossed in his recital that he sprang naked to his feet and spread his arms in a cruciform attitude at the edge of his cot. He lost his balance and fell over the side so that a wall of the canvas tent was upset, exposing them to the view of adjacent roof-tops, but worse than that, provoking in Mrs. Stone an uncontrollable burst of hilarity. Being laughed at was intolerable to Paolo, and whenever she inadvertently showed her amusement over some childish speech or action of his, he would take the most spiteful reprisal that he could think of. On this occasion the revenge was verbal and oddly feminine, for after he had restored the screen to position and regained his own naked dignity on the cot, he said to Mrs. Stone, I don't blame you for laughing. It is ridiculous of me to talk about my doves to someone who is interested only in the golden excrement of the American Eagle. But you should not imagine that you are never ridiculous yourself, because you are. You were ridiculous last night.

I am sure that I am often ridiculous, said Mrs. Stone. But what did I do last night?

You asked me if I loved you, said Paolo.

Was that ridiculous?

Beside my family and my doves, said Paolo, I have only loved one person and that was my second cousin the Principessa di Leo who was raped by drunken American soldiers in Naples and has gone into the Convent of The Grey Nuns. So laugh all you please! I don't love anybody . . .

She had placed her hand over his, but then he turned on his side so that his hand was free and his back was towards her, the flawlessly sculptured back of an outraged copper efebo, and there was an interval of hostile silence.

Speaking of birds, said Mrs. Stone with an effect of composure, is it true that the rondini don't have legs and that is the reason they stay in the air all the time?

No, said Paolo, they stay in the air all the time because they don't want to mix with American tourists.

His coolness towards Mrs. Stone persisted till late in the afternoon when they had gone to have cocktails at the Excelsior and where, as a panicky gesture of peacemaking, she had suddenly proposed that they go to a famous sartoria on the Corso d'Italia to have Paolo measured for some new clothes. He had demurred only faintly, with a coquetry that was almost girlish, and on their way to the tailor he told her that the Signora Coogan had wanted to give him a blood-red Alfa-Romeo for Christmas but that he could not accept it from her because he didn't love her. But this is different, he said, because we *love* each other!

When Mrs. Stone reminded him that earlier that same afternoon he had said it was ridiculous to ask him if he loved her, because he had loved nobody but his family and his doves and the second cousin gone into a convent, Paolo took her gloved hand. I only told you that because you had hurt my feelings. And besides, when you love somebody, you mustn't listen to what they say. They say things to hurt you because they're afraid of being hurt themselves. You must look at their eyes, said Paolo, and feel their *hearts*!

He said this with such apparent simplicity and tenderness, that Mrs. Stone burst into tears. It was only relief and happiness that made her weep, she told him. But privately she doubted that her emotion could be defined that simply.

PART TWO
ISLAND, ISLAND!

It was true that for brief intervals in her relationship with Paolo, Mrs. Stone had caught glimpses of something that she thought might be happiness. It was something she could not identify, that feeling, because she had not been acquainted with it before. She had experienced the nervous elation of triumphs in her profession, but if the play were a great success, the long run that followed was tedious and exhausting and it was only the spur of competitive ambition that kept her pursuing that kind of success. In her heart she had always been jealous of the playwrights, even the ones long dead, because for them there must have been some freedom in the creative work but for her it was only the following out of a prescribed pattern of speeches and acts. She was not a very inventive actress. In her heart she suspected her lack of illumination, and though she made a great show of exulting in the successes of other actresses, sending them bushels of roses and paeans of telegraphic praise, secretly she was pleased when their performances were not accorded the laurels given her own; only in their failures did she feel a genuine sisterly warmth towards them. When another actress had a tremendous success that equalled or surpassed her own, she would sometimes give ragged performances for a week afterwards, even forget her lines or lose her voice. Once she had insisted upon the dismissal of a subordinate player and this actress had written her a note saying, *I know why you had me fired. It was because you were upset over Helen's wonderful notices!* But in those days Mrs. Stone did not have to acknowledge unpleasant truths about herself to herself. She was kept so continually engaged in her work and the business of being an important social and theatrical personality that she did not have time, even if she had had the impulse, for examining the occult reasons of her heart. Events followed upon each other too swiftly, the interlocking pattern was too close and secure, and her prestige seemed invulnerable to her. She used to say to her husband, I suppose I would have a nervous breakdown if I had the time for it! But the power of her still youthful being was continually absorbed in the career and the social existence that kept rocketing onward, onward, with no apparent aim other than that of the motion and the velocity themselves. The failure as Juliet had come like the head-on collision of two opposite velocities, and only then did she realize that she had been racing ahead with her eyes tight shut and her fists doubled at her sides, really knowing only that she was moving, and moving swiftly. The opposite force had been time, time the imponderable, not moving amicably with her but treacherously against her, and finally meeting her and arresting her in mid-flight with a shattering crash. And then, among the ruins, she had risen to her feet with what she thought was gallant laughter and some dignity, and announced to the world, which cared a great deal less than she and her husband imagined, that she was retiring from the stage because of her husband's health, and was going with him on a long vacation to Europe and Asia.

It was true that for some time past Mr. Stone had been subject to attacks of faintness, but when one is continually rushing to keep various appointments, as Mr. and Mrs. Stone had now been doing for so many years, the idea of death as being relative to oneself and one's immediate company-in-flight is only theoretically and never *actually* acceptable. Appointments are reassuring. As long as you know where you are to go and what time you are to be there, say, the hairdresser at four o'clock, the photographer at five-thirty, the Colony at six, the theatre at seven-thirty, Sardi's at midnight and to bed at one, there is a feeling of impregnability. As long as you stay in places like those and keep such precise appointments, keep busy, keep chatting, keep rehearsing or acting, keep *going*, the old man made out of bones will surely not dare to show himself except on a certain page of the newspaper which is several pages behind the social and theatrical columns and can be deftly skipped past when you turn to the market quotations.

So Mrs. Stone had not found it necessary to take Mr. Stone's condition seriously until she used it as a pretext for closing her unsuccessful play. Their doctor had also chosen to make light of it. He told them that it was only a passing symptom of what he called "the climacteric". However, about a week before they were to sail for Europe, this doctor had invited Mrs. Stone to his office for a confidential talk, and then he had told her that the reassuring attitude he had taken was merely a part of the treatment, not a true diagnosis. He seriously doubted that the flagging heart of Mr. Stone would carry him all the way around the world and back. It was just as if he had said to her, if you will give me your itinerary I will provide you with the name of a reliable mortician in each of your ports-of-call.

Mrs. Stone had a sense of personal outrage.

Mr. Stone is *not* going to die, she said to the doctor coolly. One has a feeling about those things and if there had been any real danger of it, I would have known in my heart. I don't care what your instruments tell you. He is just a very tired man who took my career more seriously than I did, and after he's rested and relaxed a few weeks, this cardiac neurosis will disappear. I have always suspected that you doctors are in league with the undertakers and that if one of you went out of business, the other would have to follow!

She had gotten up, laughing, exercising her grand

stage manner, as she held out her white gloved hand to the doctor who was, after all, a sort of little stage-manager who had overstepped his authority in directing her, the star, in a bit of stage-business. But after she had left the doctor's office, with a list of foreign doctors that she had condescended to accept from him, her faith in the impossibility of real danger crumbled. By the time of their sailing day on the Queen Mary, that danger, that grey imminence, walked up the gangplank with them and settled itself implacably among the fancily-beribboned champagne bottles and cellophaned baskets of fruit that wished them bon voyage. It was like somebody in a room that you pretend not to see but whom you are nevertheless always looking at indirectly. She suspected that Mr. Stone, for all his display of immoderately good spirits, was equally aware of the shadow. For when he was not laughing or talking, he was continually clearing his throat or adjusting his collar or giving little nervous coughs. He smoked his cigarettes only a third of the way down and crushed them out with unnecessary violence, and his mild and curiously infantile grey eyes had a look of glassiness which was not there before, not even during the blackest time of the economic depression.

Among the things to which Mrs. Stone had not given much prior consideration was the extent and quality of her feeling for her husband, and she was at this time making the belated discovery that what she had assumed was only an ordinary attachment was actually a dependence of profound order. For it was Mr. Stone, and only Mr. Stone, who had occupied a companion-seat with her on that rocket which had carried her dizzily onward through the interstellar spaces of her career-existence. Their marriage, in its beginning, had come very close to disaster because of a sexual coldness, amounting to aversion, on her part, and a sexual awkwardness, amounting to impotence, on his. If one night, nearly twenty-five years ago, he had not broken down and wept on her breast like a baby, and in this way transferred his position from that of unsuccessful master to that of pathetic dependent, the marriage would have cracked up. But the pathos had succeeded where the desire had not. She had taken him into her arms with a sudden tenderness and the marriage had then suddenly been set right, or at least had been salvaged. Through his inadequacy Mr. Stone had allowed them both to discover what both really wanted, she an adult child and he a living and young and adorable mother.

It was only in the years following her retirement from the stage that Mrs. Stone learned to exercise a gift for candour with herself. While she was absorbed in the monomania of her profession she was necessarily less analytical of her own actions and there was once an occasion when she did something quite outrageous without daring to know why she did it. That was fifteen years ago when she was touring the country as Shakespeare's Rosalind. Orlando was played by a young actor whose good looks and lyric style were in serious competition with her own, in their scenes together she could some times feel a diversion of audience interest from herself that was increasingly provoking. Yet she had to pretend to be gratified by his success in the part and the rave notices that he was given by female reviewers who usually made some discreet comment on his remarkable adaptability to the revealing costumes of Elizabethan drama. Her tension built up steadily, until during the interval of a matinée in the city of Toledo, Mrs. Stone experienced some kind of a seizure as she passed his dressing-room and saw him seated before the mirror in a pair of apple-green tights. She entered the dressing-room and slammed the door and locked it. He turned a startled look from the mirror on which she had interrupted his Narcissean gaze. Her look was even more startled than his, for she had no idea what the purpose of her intrusion might be. Was she intending to burst into hysterical abuse? Perhaps it was the panicky notion that that might be her intention that inspired her to the only other release of emotion that she could think of, which was to envelop him in a violent embrace, which she instantly proceeded to do, in a manner that was more like a man's with a girl, and to which he submitted in a way that also suggested a reversal of gender — although finally, at the necessary moment in the embrace, she had changed to the woman's more natural pose of acceptance and he had managed to assume the (fairly well-acted) role of the aggressor. The rise of the next curtain had been delayed for fifteen minutes because there was no response from the star's dressing-room. But a night or two later, when this Orlando had attempted to repay the off-stage visit, she had said to him, without turning from her dressing-room mirror, I think what happened last Saturday can be blamed on the benzedrine drops I took in my coffee. Excuse me, I've got to change quickly.

The incident had one salutary effect. It removed him as a source of anxiety to her. Thereafter she dominated him upon the stage, obliterating him in the shadow of her virtuosity as boldly as a hawk descending upon some powerless little creature of the grasses. When Christmas was celebrated in the city of Denver she gave him an expensive leather-bound scrap-book with the legend *Rave Notices* embossed in silver on its cover. This was a delicately spiteful gift, because ever since the matinée in Toledo, his name was accorded only perfunctory mention in the press. And not long after he had huffily turned in his notice with a letter saying, *The star-system in the theatre has suffocated young talent . . .*

The Toledo incident had been lightning out of a blue sky, and a rarity that had no echo in her professional life thereafter. She was careful to replace that Orlando with one who wore russet leather and apple-green silk less distractingly, and when the tour ended, she returned to Mr. Stone with a special gratitude, as a child awakens from a frightening dream to encircle the throat of its mother. She had given no direct thought of the ignobility of her behaviour towards the young actor: it had not consciously struck her that she had behaved like a great bird of plunder. In her, nevertheless, was something that recoiled from her conduct and was shaken by it. She needed Mr. Stone to reassure her that nothing dreadful had happened. She told him about the incident in the dressing-room, and that evening he said to her, I know that I haven't ever made love to you really satisfactorily. For it was, of course, the sexual side of the incident that had impressed him, not the far more significant question of ethics. Mr. Stone gave her absolution only for the carnal incident; but she pretended, with him, that this was all that there really was to understand and forgive, and she, in return, had reassured him, and with considerable truth, that their own relations had been and still were what she desired, that the lightning-like episode came from no cloud of latent dissatisfaction. And on the night that followed, it was she that took comfort from him, for the role of child and mother is curiously interchangeable when it becomes the basis of an adult marriage.

The marriage of the Stones was haunted by a mysterious loneliness. All substitute relationships are haunted by something like that. The desiring fingers enclose a phantom object, the hungering lips are pressed to a ghostly mouth. The mother lies in the grave and the child is not born, but in the very act of substitution there is a particular tenderness of pathos. Perhaps if they had not interrupted the pattern of their career-existence in New York, that pathos would have remained something on the very margin of consciousness, amorphous as some child she had never borne; but with the interruption of pattern that came with the long sea voyage, the dissociation from all of the protective distractions of theatres and offices and society, that haunting insufficiency, that loneliness, became as visible as breath that turns to vapour. It became a grey mist floating between them through which they exchanged their eagerly denying smiles at each other and their reassuring light speeches.

They had intended to take a leisurely world-tour, in fact, all of the boat and plane and hotel bookings had been made in advance. But when they had returned from the theatre one night in Paris, when Mr. Stone had gone into the bathroom to brush his teeth, the commonplace sound of the brushing had been interrupted by a series of hoarse inhuman noises of strangulation. Mrs. Stone had rushed to the bathroom to find his body sagging to the floor and the short, plump hands clinging to the edge of the washbowl as if it were that support of white porcelain that offered him his only remaining hold on a state of being. He survived that attack, as he had several previous, but it decided them that travel was at present too strenuous and that it would be better to settle down somewhere for a time. After

Mr. Stone had rested a few days in a Paris clinic, they had flown south to Rome.

During the stay in Rome there was an encouraging remission in Mr. Stone's illness, and it was during that remission that she had accompanied him one afternoon to the world-famous tailor on the Corso d'Italia to have him measured for some new clothes, not because he needed or wanted any, but more as a token of confidence that he would live to wear them.

* * *

Now returning to this same tailor with Paolo, Mrs. Stone recalled how she and her husband had smiled at each other across the sunny office while the measurements were made of Mr. Stone's rather ridiculous plump figure. They had selected for him a suit of dove-grey flannel. Now from one of his glass cabinets the same tailor was producing a bolt of this same material and unrolling it upon the bare display table.

Come and feel it, he said to Mrs. Stone.

No, said Mrs. Stone. I know how it feels . . .

She turned instantly away from the table and pretended to notice for the first time the potted bush of white azaleas on the window-seat: for it was in Mr. Stone's suit of dove-grey flannel that he had suffered his final attack of anguish and suffocation aboard a plane that was bearing them towards Athens. Now with her back to Paolo and the tailor,

73

she recalled that awful parting above the earth in a
storm of brassy light and mechanical sound. She
remembered looking across the narrow aisle of the
plane and seeing that the small, plump body of her
husband had grown unnaturally rigid and that the
knuckles of his hands were clutching the side-arms
of the chair as if it were they, and only they, that
kept him from falling all that dizzy blue distance
into the Ionian sea that they were flying over. She
remembered leaning a little forward and sidewise,
and saying to him with gentle hesitation, Tom, are
you feeling badly? And she remembered the tight,
quick jerk of his head in denial, which she knew
was a lie. She remembered looking at the tiny
platinum band on her wrist which indicated the
meridian of the day and the suddenly atrocious fact
that it would be three hours before this incredibly
soaring but lifeless bird that bore them through
space would deposit them back upon the earth
again. And she had then leaned in the other direction and stared below them, through the curved
pane of glass and the dazzling vacuity of air, down
to the still more dazzling and vacant-looking
expanse of the sea, and she had noted (and only
then cried out) that not far away, a little to the north
of their course of flight, was a tiny island with some
white buildings on it. Her cry was to the stewardess.

*Tell the pilot he's got to make a landing! My
husband is ill!*

And even then Mr. Stone had turned and smiled
denyingly at her and he had said something to her

that was lost in the mechanical bird's great continual voice. Then for a few moments the stewardess had stood between her and her husband, bending solicitously over him, so that Mrs. Stone could see only the pinkish crown of his head, and in that tiny space of visual separation, as though the young lady had reached down horribly quickly and efficiently under his dove-grey vest and snatched his heart away from him, Mr. Stone had ceased being alive. If the cool young stewardess in the grey uniform had not stood between and so disconnected the supporting thread of their fused gaze upon each other, Mrs. Stone felt that it might not have happened, the death, so when the young woman had turned back towards her, saying, *Your husband has fainted*, she sprang from her seat and thrust her hands wildly against the young woman's breast and belly, pushing her violently away and screaming confused things at her until she had forced her almost to the door of the pilot's compartment and then she, Mrs. Stone, had turned back to restore her husband to the world that this intruder had snatched him out of. But she had known instantly by the way that the plump little body was collapsing into its soft grey flannel suiting, that the thing gone from it was not retrievable now. The brilliantly vacuous air was what now contained it. Then she had been all screaming voice and imploring arms, trying to fight her way past the strong young stewardess to the compartment of the pilot, to the glazed and corrugated grey metal of that doorway, crying

75

out, *Island, Island!* And finally, because the girl, and a grey-uniformed young man who emerged from the front compartment, could not seem to understand what the word *island* meant, she had thrown herself into a vacant seat nearer the front of the plane and beat her wing-like arms on the pane of glass that looked over the sea and the bit of green island now gliding serenely beneath them and behind them.

Madam, they said to her gently, *there is no possible landing on that island . . .*

* * *

Paolo ordered not only a suit of dove-grey flannel, but two others, a midnight blue tuxedo and a suit of shantung silk the colour of a yellow pearl.

Mrs. Stone had never seen, even in a child, such a degree of excitement as he exhibited at the tailor's. He talked with his head thrown so far back that his throat seemed in danger of snapping, and he continuously gesticulated with a hand held before him in the form of a fiercely closed cup.

Strette, strette, strette, he yelled to the tailor as the measurement of his superb young body was taken.

While all this violence and computation was going on, Mrs. Stone retired to a lonely corner of the room, outside of the betraying sunlight, and surrendered herself not to memory any more but to the still more dismaying process of reflection. She tried to understand how she had arrived where she was. Perhaps there existed some logical but secret continuity between her past career-existence in America and this anomalous sequel to it that was now unfolding in Rome, and if she sat here long enough, in reflective privacy, the plausible line of development might show itself to her. Surely somewhere along the course of her progress, from the fairly ordinary gentility of her girlhood in Virginia and those school-dramatics which had led into the choice of her profession, and then through the obsessive pursuit of that profession and through the years of conventional marriage, surely somewhere along that terribly rapid but uniform course, there lay some token, however cryptic, some inconspicuous sign-post that pointed towards Paolo and this spring in Rome. There were all the various integers and symbols of the long equation, arranged in their temporal sequence across the page, but the equation halted without a summation. To say it halted was, of course, not exact. It was, in a way, still continuing. If she herself had died on the plane to Athens, for instance, the equation would have been more cleanly cut off, though still without a summation. Something had indeed halted, all that part of her life that composed the orderly set of integers and symbols, all that had come to a close, but she was going on somehow, still being, still watching and sensing and knowing as before, indeed more vividly, now, than she had in the past when the kind of emotional anarchy which now seemed to possess her had happened only twice, in a college dormitory and the dressing-room in Toledo, and the not quite, but —

* * *

Mrs. Stone abruptly looked up from her white gloves. The voices of the tailor and Paolo had receded into a further display room but it was not the recession of that sound but the intrusion of another that had caught her attention. There was a metallic tapping audible in the room. For a moment she did not know where it came from. Then she abruptly caught sight of the young man's figure standing just outside the glass window that fronted the office. He did not seem to be looking into the window but down at the hand held in front of him with which he was rapping upon the glass with something metallic. The face was so inclined that she might not have recognized it as the face dimly seen on so many recent occasions as she came and went about the streets of the city, but the curiously secretive and yet bold attitude of the figure she knew at once to be his. It was the attitude of someone in a crowd who is intent upon attracting the attention of a single person without betraying his signal to any other. Although the afternoon was warm, the collar of his top-coat was turned up about his throat and his face lowered to be in its shadow, and as he continued the faint, barely audible, tapping, he gave short, furtive glances in each direction along the sunny walk. Then with a barely noticeable gesture he divided the unbuttoned front of his coat by a couple of inches and Mrs. Stone's aghast look caught the flash of outrageous nudity which the slight motion exposed. Instantly she got up from the chair and turned to the row of glass cabinets along the back wall. She remained facing that way for several moments. The rapping ceased and in the flawed reflection of the cabinet glass she saw the figure moving away from the window. Then she called out to the men in the further display room. She called out to them in a tone of alarm, but when Paolo answered, she was somehow ashamed to say what had happened but only remarked that they must hurry to keep an appointment for dinner.

PART THREE

THE DRIFT

When Mrs. Stone was a child of ten her parents had separated and the little girl was sent to a boarding-school in Maryland. At that time she had not played much with children, she was very adult and prissy, admired by the teachers for her ladylike deportment, her golden curls and enormous violet eyes. She was more like a picture of a melancholy little princess than an actual child. With her hands in her lap and her ankles daintily crossed, she would appear to be posing for a portrait by a romantic Victorian painter. She held her lips rather tightly together and she looked rapidly about her without turning her head, so that sometimes, in spite of her fairytale beauty, she looked rather cold and sly. The other little girls did not take kindly to her. Several abusing little nicknames were invented for her, such as Miss Priss or The Pet. This hostility did not seem to surprise the little girl. You would have supposed that it was exactly what her past experience, limited as it was, had led her to expect of associates in the world-away-from-home. After a while, as though she had carefully thought the situation out, she pinned up her long golden curls and discarded her ladylike postures and began to look and behave like the other children. But she was always like a little grown-up imitating a child rather than actually being one. And the beauty was ineradicable. Only a great deal of time could modify that.

By midwinter of her first year at the school Karen had gone to the other extreme of behaviour. She had turned into a tomboy and was outstanding in competitive games and sports. On the lawn of the school there was a very steep terrace which was difficult to scale when it was coated with ice or banked with snow. At those times the rowdier little girls, such as Karen, would often play a game called King On The Mountain. In this game, which was not sanctioned and was later forbidden by the faculty, a single child would take a position on the height of the terrace and hold the title of King On The Mountain as long as she prevented any other from climbing to her level. This was one of those games at which the new character of Karen showed to great advantage. She was the most tenacious holder of the citadel. She was also the most ferocious of the besiegers. The game would often break up in a tumult of torn clothes, bruises and tears, but with Karen triumphantly planted at the summit of the slippery incline.

King On The Mountain was not a game that she had discarded with the passing of childhood. Her adult methods of playing it had naturally undergone a very marked revolution. Scrambling, pushing, kicking and scratching had been replaced by ostensibly civilized tactics. But Mrs. Stone's arrival at the height of her profession, and the heroic tenacity with which she held that position against all besieging elements or persons, with the sole exception of time, could not fail to impress Mrs. Stone as having a parallel to the childhood game on the terrace. At certain unguarded moments, those moments when the cultivated adult self, quickly and covertly as two thieves pass between them a stolen watch, receives a transmission from its original, natural being, she had intercepted the inner whisper of these exultant words: *I am still King On The Mountain!*

Politics had taken the place of childhood violence. Mrs. Stone's great tours about the country as a star resembled the conduct of a campaign for government office. Politicians make a special point of remembering names and faces. So did Mrs. Stone. There were literally hundreds of people she knew and called by their first names though they were mere acquaintances. In every city on the big touring circuit she knew practically everything there was to be known about every columnist or reviewer, things such as defective eyesight or hearing which made it advisable to plant them in the front of the house, their preference for a certain type of liquor, their particular little vanities and concerns. If they had put on excessive weight since she had last seen them, she would say, Oh, my, how thin you've gotten. And if one of them, as happened not infrequently, had a secret susceptibility to members of his own sex, there was always someone in her company that she could make a discreet point of introducing him to. She understood and was tolerant of so much. She was never sharp or catty. The old trick of glancing about very quickly, without moving her head, the childhood trick which had made her seem cold and sly, was put to excellent use on all occasions. She saw and knew so much, and what she didn't know was known by her secretary. Their file of information, between the two of them, was simply staggering. Usually her first question of the day to this spinster secretary was, Whose birthday is it? There was a notebook entirely devoted to dates of nativity covering a vast range of persons, from former President's widow to a sob sister on *The Tulsa Gazette*. Whose birthday is it, she would inquire, or who died today? Both questions were asked in precisely the same tone of dispassionate, almost scientific, interest. There was a continual flow of congratulatory greetings and messages of condolence, and Flora, the goddess of Springtime, was not more lavish in a dispersal of flowers. Two mornings each week were devoted to hospital calls. If the humblest member of the stage-crew took sick, he could count on Mrs. Stone's visit whether he desired it or not. There was nothing, it must be admitted, very cheering about these hospital visits of hers. She looked at sick people with the hard eyes of a bird and her sympathetic tones were produced from her throat. Victims of incurable malignancies touched her no more deeply than those recovering from the removal of tonsils. Everything that she did to court the favour of her professional associates, to create the legend of Mrs. Stone as a paragon of loyalty and goodness, was directed by the head as distinguished from the heart. The result was that a great many people said *Mrs. Stone is a wonderful woman* in almost the same perfunctory tones with which she inquired of her secretary, Who died today, or Whose birthday is it?

Nobody was more aware of the automatic quality of her gestures than Mrs. Stone herself. This was something she neither condemned in herself nor condoned. She knew that she loved two things, Tom Stone and her career as an actress and she decided, perhaps quite sensibly, that it did not particularly matter if her show of concern for others came from the heart or the head. It did matter, however, that as time went on the birdlike opacity of her eyes and the voice that simulated an emotion not felt began to show more plainly through the gradually collapsing fortification of beauty which had helped so much to make her *King On The Mountain*. Mrs. Stone *knew* it. She did not fail to discover this creeping attrition and to do everything in her power to compensate for it by increased exercise of skill.

Mrs. Stone was what is called a "quick study". She was really somewhat ashamed of the phenomenal rapidity with which she learned her speeches, for it is customary in the theatre for the important stars to take their time about committing parts to memory. Ambition and anxiety would not allow Mrs. Stone to take her time about anything connected with her profession. Often she would know her "sides" after three or four rehearsals. It disturbed her to think that this rapidity might be construed as the sign of efficiency as distinguished from art. For that reason she would often pretend to stumble over lines that she knew perfectly well. There was also this advantage. Behind the cover of a false incompetence, Mrs. Stone could keep a needle-sharp eye on other members of the company who might threaten to outshine her when the play was open.

Of course these things could escape detection for only a limited time. Despite her efforts to conceal her efficiency, it became legendary in the theatre. Finally everyone who knew her, knew what she was up to. She was up to being, and keeping on being, King On The Mountain. So long as she continued to possess her beauty, this was all very well. But when that beauty passed, the tell tale glints of a finely-grooved mechanism, highly oiled, began to be apparent. Then the observations that "Mrs. Stone was not at her best last night" or "Mrs. Stone is brilliant but slightly miscast in the role of" began to sound the death-rattle of a career to which something in her had never been altogether suited. This being the case, there was some mystery in the vehemence with which she pursued her career. But there was also a mystery in the unmaidenly violence with which she used to play King On The Mountain in her long ago childhood. But perhaps there is that same mystifying element in all human urgencies. Knowing the reason for something, or anything, is not common knowledge . . .

All those things she remembered, all those names and faces and characteristics of people who might conceivably be of use to her, were like articles stored on shelves about the walls of some great vacant chamber. This vacancy was not the vacancy of a trivial person. Mrs. Stone knew what that sort of vacancy was, as well as anyone knows it. It was that sort of vacancy which permitted so many people of her acquaintance to lead the sort of lives they led without any evident consciousness of taking part in a vast ritual of nothingness. Mrs. Stone knew of that ritual. She took part in it herself. She went to the parties; she pursued the little diversions. She moved in the great, empty circle. But Mrs. Stone glanced inward from the peripheries of that circle and saw the void enclosed there. She saw the emptiness. She knew that it was empty. But Mrs. Stone was always a busy woman. She had been continually occupied with more things than a single existence seemed sufficient to hold, and for that reason, the way that centrifugal force prevents a whirling object from falling inward from its orbit, Mrs. Stone was removed for a long time from the void she circled.

When she retired from the stage and sailed from America with her dying husband, and with a body which had chosen that time to declare itself no longer eligible for that service to life which it had never served, Mrs. Stone knew, in her heart, that she was turning boldly inward from the now slackened orbit, turning inward and beginning, now, to enter the space enclosed by the path of passionate flight. She knew it in her heart without consciously knowing it. And being a person of remarkable audacity, she moved inward with her violet eyes wide open, asking herself, in her heart, what would she find as she moved? Was it simply a void, or did it contain some immaterial force that still might save as well as it might destroy her?

One late spring afternoon Mrs. Stone made the startling discovery that a great storm had blown into the storeplaces of her mind and scattered all those names and faces to the four winds and the seven corners. She had just alighted from her car at a kerbstone on Via Veneto and was preparing to enter the shop of a dressmaker when a woman's voice hailed her by the name of Karen. An instant later her arm was seized by someone she had only the vaguest recollection of having seen somewhere before. She covered up her failure of recollection with rapid small talk, but it was several minutes before it dawned upon her that this was not a mere acquaintance. This was someone who had belonged to that inner circle of friends that the Stones thought of as "their crowd". It was Julia McIlhenny and her male companion, the great toad-like man hovering uncomfortably behind a cigar, was a former business-associate, a man who had invariably "bought into" Mrs. Stone's productions. She had not recognized them. Not for several minutes had she the ghost of an idea who they were. When it came to her, the enormity of this lapse, it unnerved her. Tears welled into her eyes. Oh, Julia, she murmured, remembering at last the name of the plump little woman. Julia, there is something I have to tell you. And then, drawing the woman aside, away from her husband, Mrs. Stone, for some unfathomable reason, began to invent a lie about herself. She told the woman that she was afflicted with a malignant growth, that she had undergone an operation for it, but that the growth had returned. She could not live long. When the woman said *where*, or perhaps only when it seemed to Mrs. Stone that she had asked *where*, she told her that it was a growth in the womb. She told her that the womb had been removed but that the growth was too far advanced and had extended by metastasis to other organs. While she invented this lie about herself, Mrs. Stone felt something resembling joy, a sense of wild freedom that she had known only occasionally at moments on the stage when her virtuosity overcame, all at once, the difficulties of a complex role. The sense of liberation continued even after she left the woman, gasping, beginning to weep, at the sidewalk café where the encounter took place. Don't call me, don't try to see me, she cried at parting. I know you will understand that I can't see people!

Instead of going into the dressmaker's shop, which would have been a little unsuitable after such a story, she returned to her car and had the driver drive her about the Villa Borghese for a while. Over and over, she had repeated delightedly to herself, *Just think, I didn't know them! Ha! Think of that, I didn't even know them . . .*

For that was the aspect of the curious incident which impressed her, at first, as being most significant. Only later, when the driver turned to inquire if she'd had enough of the park, did it strike her as being equally notable that she had, out of nowhere, apparently, caught hold of such a fantastic lie about herself. No, she said to the driver, keep on going. She leaned back in the leather cushions, and as the car twisted at random among the devious ways of the Villa Borghese, Mrs. Stone had a sense of arrival. This was the centre. This was what the frantic circles surrounded. *Here* was the *void . . .*

★   ★   ★

Like most persons possessed of unusual beauty, Mrs. Stone had long entertained the romantic notion that she would die early. In her girlhood she had expected to die before thirty. Later on the limit had been advanced to forty-five or fifty, but now that she had passed both of these temporal extremities, the idea of an early death was exposed as a mere conceit which fate had no intention of gratifying. It could not be said that she really wanted to die. It could only be said that she was alarmed by the direction, or lack of direction, that her life was now taking. If she had known that she was actually suffering from any such pathological condition as the one that she had invented for Mrs. McIlhenny's astonishment, some disease that could not be cured and which would eventuate in death at a reasonably early date, this knowledge might actually have had a pacifying effect. But such was not the case. Her body showed none of those symptoms of an organism which is about to run down. The debility, the shortness of breath, the erratic pulse of a middle-aged person marked for a fairly early demise were altogether lacking in Mrs. Stone's constitution. On the contrary, now that her body was rising out of the tangled woods of the climacteric, she felt a great resurgence of physical well-being. She was continually active without ever becoming quite tired. Other Americans complained of the Roman languor, but Mrs. Stone had not experienced anything of that sort. She wished that she had. Often she wished that she had the physical lassitude that would make an afternoon in bed seem attractive to her. Yes, it was possible to lie still. Her body would consent to it if the command were given. But if she were lying there alone, if Paolo was not beside her, at once she would feel a torment of restlessness. She would get up to fasten the shutters or pick up a bit of lingerie that had slipped to the floor. Or she would imagine that she was thirsty or she would remember something that she had meant to tell the maid or the butler to do, and a few moments later she would be back on her feet again; and when the trivial business was completed, to look again at the white solitude of the bed would give her a feeling of positive revulsion. Usually she would sit beside the phone, sometimes with a hand resting on the receiver but seldom actually lifting it from the hook. Even when she lifted it, with a finger poised to dial the five numbers which might or might not invoke the languid response of Paolo, his sleepy Pronto, her resolution would fail and the uncertain hand would replace the instrument and fall back into her lap or fasten idly upon a tumbler of water or a bottle of scent.

No doubt the trouble was partly that Mrs. Stone had failed to make any intellectual provisions for the time of life that now confronted her. For many years the only reading that had really interested her was play manuscripts and theatrical columns of newspapers. She enjoyed music only as a background to some activity such as bathing or dressing. The cataclysmic period of history through which she had lived, making of wars and the mighty struggle of social ideas, had been as immaterial to her as a crowd of anonymous faces passed on the street. It was all a faintly variable blur that did not concern her unless it happened to brush her shoulder or momentarily deter her own determined but almost unthinking progress past and through it.

From these facts about Mrs. Stone it would be easy to assume that she was a stupid woman, but like most quick and easy deductions of human character, this was not quite the truth. There are cases in which a great deal of energy is a detriment to intelligence, and this is especially true when all, or practically all, of that energy is devoted to a single thing, such as the obsessive pursuit of a career. If a fairly keen intelligence had not been involved in this pursuit, she would not have ultimately seen through it with such merciless clarity, such clarity as that which had allowed her to admit to herself that her talent had been second-rate and that the pediment of her career had been youthful beauty which was now removed from her. It takes a kind of intelligence to acknowledge such a merciless truth concerning oneself and even more to survive the acknowledgement of it. Now she knew, and now she was still going on, and not merely going on but going on with unchecked audacity and a surprising amount of enjoyment. Her physical hardihood portended at least twenty more years of existence, not merely as a middle-aged but as an elderly woman, and it was, of course, dismaying, on brilliant spring mornings, to face the mirror in her bedroom with the sort of realism that still redeemed her from being a commonplace person. She was obliged to witness that her face in the mirror had not weathered the critical period just passed through so triumphantly as had the organs that kept her living. Her body had flown like a powerful bird through and

95

above the entangling branches of the past few years, but her face now exhibited the record of the flight.

A number of times lately Mrs. Stone had gone out on the street in make-up applied almost as artfully as that she had worn on the stage, but Roman sunlight was not in sympathy with the deceit, and she was aware of receiving glances that were not merely critical but sometimes mocking. She had her hair tinted a darker shade, almost auburn, and she took to wearing hats with very wide brims of gossamer material that filtered the light in a flattering way, but at the back of her mind was continually the shadow of a suspicion, not yet resolved into thought, that something more radical than any of these expedients must rather sooner than later be contrived to prepare her for that long crossing of time that apparently still lay before her . . .

Mrs. Stone was now spending a great deal of money on clothes at the Roman branches of the great Parisian dressmakers. In the days of her unfaded beauty she had preferred simple clothes and a single ring, but her taste had now shifted to gowns and jewellery that seemed inspired by the baroque façades of Bernini. Among them was a dinner gown of golden taffeta covered with ivory lace with which she wore several ornate rings and a necklace of pearls and topaz, and she was trying on this particular costume for the first time one afternoon when Paolo burst into her bedroom wearing the completed dove-grey flannel suit that he had just that day received from the tailor.

It was perhaps unreasonable of her to expect Paolo to be interested in her own finery, but if he had only paused in the doorway long enough to show some agreeable surprise at her appearance, the evening might not have turned out so disastrously. But Paolo's agreeable surprise was reserved for his own appearance. He rushed toward the mirror as if it were water and his clothes were on fire. Without a glance in Mrs. Stone's direction, he gazed and preened in the glass, and finding it somewhat crowded by their two reflections, he murmured *Excuse me* and gave her a slight push to one side. Then he turned his back to the long mirror and, looking over his shoulder, he lifted the jacket over his hips so that they both, she and he, could admire the way that the flannel adhered to the classic callipygian shape of his firm young behind.

At this point Mrs. Stone burst into laughter which was not mirthful but verging on desperation. Paolo went into an instant fury. He snatched out his American cigarettes and marched into the bathroom, to the smaller but more private mirror over the washbowl, calling back to her, *I am not used to wearing such fine new clothes!* And then he slammed the door shut.

There is thirty years' difference between us, thought Mrs. Stone.

Then she was ashamed of herself and by the time Paolo had emerged from the bathroom she had mixed two negronis and placed them on the glass-topped table on the still sunny terrace with a bowl of olives between. Paolo came outside with an air of abstraction. He paid no attention to the drinks, but left her sipping hers while he wandered over to the balustrade and looked moodily down into the little piazza at the top of the Spanish Steps. Mrs. Stone thought to herself, This is a time to lie low. And so she made no comment. She sipped her drink with her eyes on his grey flannel back and she thought of the night when the flannel would not stand between them.

But all at once Paolo turned and asked her a startling question.

Who is this boy that follows you all the time lately?

What! Who?

Haven't you noticed him? He keeps behind us almost wherever we go. He's down there now, at the top of the Spanish stairs. Look down there!

She rose and joined him at the balustrade, but she could not look down for more than a second. The sheer drop made her eyes flinch and her head whirl a little.

I cannot look down that wall, she said to Paolo. Besides, I'm sure it is only some money-changer . . .

The trouble, said Paolo darkly, is that you have made a spectacle of yourself!

Why, what do you mean!

A spectacle, said Paolo, is something that is

conspicuous, that's you! We are being pointed out on the streets! Don't you know that?

Yes, I know that, returned Mrs. Stone. And I also know that you seem to be pleased by it! Why do you always insist that the car let us out directly in front of Doney's where everyone sitting at the sidewalk tables can see and hear you while you stand there shouting idiotic instructions to the driver? It's you that likes to show off, and it's you they look at mostly, not me, not me! I don't cut nearly so fine and conspicuous a figure! Why, if you and I were playing a scene together on the stage, I wouldn't be noticed!

You don't hear the comments, said Paolo.

Oh, yes, I do, said Mrs. Stone. My ear for Italian is better than you think. "Che bel' uomo, che bel' uomo!", is what they all say at the sidewalk tables, and you bask in it like a sunflower. When we're alone together you're so lazy and sulky you'll barely talk, but the moment you find yourself in front of a crowd, you light up, you throw back your head and toss your hair and shout orders. So don't reproach me for being conspicuous, caro mio. I am only conspicuous when you make us so!

I have never, said Paolo, met an American woman who would admit that she was wrong about anything, so it is no use contradicting you. But I will repeat that you don't hear all of the comments because your ear for Italian is not as good as you think. I didn't tell you this, I wanted to avoid it, but last week I was compelled to challenge a man to a duel on account of a remark that was made about us.

What remark?

A disgusting remark!

You fought a *duel*?

I delivered a challenge and the man left Rome!

Mrs. Stone did not bother to disguise her incredulous smile at this chapter from Graustark and Paolo went on more angrily than ever.

I don't suppose it has occurred to you that women of your kind are often found murdered in bed? Well, they are, let me tell you, and there was a case last week on the French Riviera. A middle-aged woman was found in bed with her throat cut from ear to ear, almost decapitated. She was lying on the right side of the bed and there were stains of hair-oil on the other pillow. No broken lock, no forced entrance. Obviously the murderer had been brought in by the lady and gone to bed with — voluntarily!

Does this mean, said Mrs. Stone, that you are likely to kill me?

That's right, make a joke and be funny, but three or four years from now I shall pick up the paper and read an account of your death under those same circumstances!

Three or four years, said Mrs. Stone, is all the time that I want. After that a cut throat would be a convenience . . .

She laughed and thrust his drink towards him, murmuring, Stai tranquillo, but he shoved the drink away so roughly that it splashed the front of her

gown. Mrs. Stone burst into childish tears and fled
to her bedroom. A few moments later he followed
there to offer a perfunctory apology and a still more
perfunctory caress. He gave her his mouth to kiss
and allowed her hands to indulge their resistless
craving to hold him, but after a while he murmured,
I want to take off my grandmother's locket first.
And Mrs. Stone, who had no need or desire for self-
flagellation, thought it the better part of wisdom not
to inquire why the locket should not stay on . . .

The evening progressed through its appointed
stages without once breaking the steady downward
curve of Mrs. Stone's spirit into helpless anxiety nor
Paolo's humour into taciturn sulking.

At Rosati's they met some friends for cocktails.
The people were strangers to Mrs. Stone. She barely
saw them through the blur of her incipient panic
and she did not hear their conversation, only their
laughter, which struck her as being obliquely
directed at herself. She was unable to talk and Paolo
refused to. He stuck out his under lip and made
languorous eyes, not at anyone present but some
invisible creature of the air. A girl at the table made
a great fuss over him. She fished the cherry out of
her cocktail and tried to thrust it into Paolo's mouth.
He made the little throat noises of a cross baby as
he twisted his face petulantly away from the sweet
offering. The girl persisted. She forced the cherry
into his mouth. He closed his white teeth on her
fingers. She cried out in delighted pretence of pain.

Her face was suffused, her fingers stayed in his mouth and his eyes remained barely open as he continued to make the little babylike noises in his throat while one of his hands lolled caressingly in his lap.

Mrs. Stone could endure no more. She rose abruptly from the table without a word of excuse and walked to the front of the bar. There she looked back. Apparently no one had noticed her withdrawal. The little game of the cherry was still going on and the others sat about it in a circle of vicarious entrancement. The waiters watched and smiled. A man playing a violin approached the table and the pretty girl's head leaned further towards Paolo so that her hair, a little darker than honey, cascaded over her face and brushed against his, and beneath the table their legs twisted voluptuously together and the hand that had lolled caressingly in his own lap had now moved to hers. No one cared, no one objected. No one was aware that Mrs. Stone had gotten up from the table, least of all the violin which celebrated only the sweet play of youth . . .

Feeling that she was about to faint, Mrs. Stone rushed from the building. She stood for a few moments just outside the door in the amethyst light of prima sera. In her breast was the same suffocating weight that she had felt in the wings of the theatre the awful first night of Juliet, when suddenly she had known that she couldn't play it, not for all the white satin and pearls that she had decked herself with. The illusion had failed. Whispering shadows divided before her as she swept from the stage. Something caught on something. There was a rattling cascade of pearls to the floor. Idiot, she cried to the woman dressing her. The pearls cracked under her slippers, the woman began to cry, the whispering shadows seethed about her like demons of some dim inferno and now it was time to go on again but the costume was not yet adjusted. Two people were plucking at her. Now three. There was the entrance cue. Wait, wait, wait, someone whispered. She turned furiously about and struck at the detaining arms, and then she swept away from them, proudly and desperately, swept back into the pale blue gelatin flood of light on the stage where failure was being carved like a monument of stone with each line and gesture of the ridiculously unsuitable part for a middle-aged woman to play . . .

What does that matter now, thought Mrs. Stone, and she thought it so forcibly that her lips murmured the words.

All at once, as if in response to her murmur, she heard a little sound of metallic tapping. She did not turn her head. The tapping came from only a few feet away on the other side of the doorway by which she was standing. A tall figure stood there. He faced the interior of the building. His head was inclined as if he were looking down at the metal object with which he was rapping the glass but it was she that the secretive tapping addressed. Mrs. Stone felt powerless to move. A pair of youths strolled by and the tapping stopped a few moments. Then it resumed again, a little bit louder. The air of the amethyst dusk became a powerful current that swept her towards him, but she did not look at him. Without looking at him, she thrust her face close to his.

Look at my face! she whispered shrilly. Why do you follow me, can't you see my face?

The youth drew back as she thrust her head towards him. He murmured something indistinguishable and turned about and began to move up the walk with his head hunched down in the collar of his coat. A little further he paused again as if he were waiting for her to join him there.

At that moment Paolo came out of the bar.

Why did you leave the table?

Please call my car, she whispered.

They drove in silence through the Villa Borghese. She leaned her head back against the leather cushion of the opened convertible until it seemed that the wave of mysterious panic had gone past, and then she directed the driver to a restaurant in Trastevere, at the same time, surreptitiously, placing on her tongue a small white tablet of belladonna. Paolo was as distant as the cold spring moon during this drive. He sat far down in the seat with his hands in his pockets. The knees of his long flannel-draped legs flopped indolently apart like the wings of a tired butterfly. As they were crossing the Tiber she dared to reach out and placed her hand upon the

knee that was near her. He accepted the touch
without response to it.

At the restaurant, Alfredo's, they dined outside.
Nervous fatigue had made her voraciously hungry
but they had hardly begun to eat when Paolo
emerged from his wordless sulking with a violent
exclamation:

My God! Have you forgotten?

What, Paolo?

You invited the Contessa and some friends to
look at our moving-pictures!

I invited?

You invited, or *I* invited! What difference does it
make? They will be there in five minutes with no
one but the butler to let them in!

Where?

At your apartment! Where do you suppose?

She started to protest, but he had already risen
and crossed away from the table. There was nothing
for her to do but pay the check and follow him out
to the car. It was the most insufferable piece of
rudeness to which she had ever been exposed,
thought Mrs. Stone.

That was probably true.

The problem of keeping her dignity was not one
that she had been forced to consider much in the
past. In the arrogance of her beauty and her prestige
in two worlds, theatrical and social, that dignity had
seemed beyond the danger of compromise; but with
the decline of her beauty and her removal from
those spheres in which she had been a person of

inviolable eminence, there was left her no protection but that of wealth: and wealth does not insure dignity. It had certainly not insured the dignity of the Signora Coogan, if accounts of that lady's conduct were to be credited. Repeatedly Mrs. Stone said to herself, on recent occasions, I am not going to lose my dignity, no matter what happens I am not going to lose it, but just as continually she caught herself doing things that were not at all consistent with that resolve. For instance one evening when Paolo was expected, she had removed from the stored-away luggage of the late Mr. Stone that great mass of theatrical mementoes which he had kept as a record of her career. There were photographs of herself in all the great parts she had played, down to and including the final unfortunate portrayal of Juliet, which only the late Mr. Stone had thought to be a notable and memorable performance and which he had dotingly insisted was the greatest of her career. As she removed that particular photograph from Mr. Stone's collection, she recalled the indignant letter she had caught him dictating to his secretary, the day the unkind notices came out. It was addressed to the one critic who had been so unchivalrous as to intimate that Mrs. Stone's limitations in the part had some relation to the age at which she played it. She had refused to let the protest go out, but now, clipped to the back of the costume photograph was this letter signed by *Thomas J. Stone* and dated two months before the time of his death. Hastily she unclipped the letter from the photograph. She stared hard at the picture of herself in her last theatrical role. It had been taken at a dress rehearsal when the nerves are at fever-pitch, but was that sufficient to account for the somehow rapacious glare, not lustre, with which the eyes, beneath a diffuse cloud of blonde hair and pearls, returned the comparatively shy gaze of the camera? The face was in rather soft focus, but even so, was there not something hawklike in its expression? As if she were about to discover some carefully guarded secret about herself, Mrs. Stone started towards the mirror with the photograph in her hand, but half way there she turned back and slipped the picture, like a card of ill omen, into the bottom of the pile. In addition to the pictures, of which there were hundreds, she found Mr. Stone's collection of theatre-programmes of all the plays she had ever appeared in, her name printed in big type over the smaller type of great play titles, and she found an immense miscellany of newspaper and magazine clippings dating from twenty-five years ago, long before she had become Mrs. Stone. Her two arms could barely support this mountain of mementoes as she carried them to the big refectory table in the middle of the sala, where Paolo could not help noticing them when he entered. Then, at the last moment, after the bell that announced Paolo from below, the indignity of such an appeal for respect had overwhelmed her with shame. She had swept the whole lot up in her arms again and rushed back to the storeroom with it. Two or three of the magnificent costume pictures had slipped from her grasp and fallen to the floor. They had lain directly in Paolo's path as he crossed from the door, and he had picked them up and tossed them onto the table with barely a glance and no comment.

Now as the car was returning them to her apartment she was desperately repeating to herself that resolution, I am not going to lose my dignity no matter what happens! But the instant that Paolo suddenly leaned over and brushed her averted cheek with his warm young mouth, she turned all her body towards him and caught both his glittering temples between her palms and cried out to him, Paolo, Paolo, I am not the Signora Coogan, I am not a wretched old fool of a woman with five hairs and two teeth in her head and nothing but money to give you!

I don't know what you are talking about, said Paolo uncomfortably.

The degree of her intensity had alarmed him.

But she would not let go. He twisted his head but she retained her hold on the polished and perfumed wings of black hair at his temples.

Look at me, Paolo, she insisted.

What for? What is the matter?

I want you to see that I am not really like that, not even when I am tired and have lost all my dignity, I am not *quite* like that!

I have not said that you were like anything at all!

It's how you have treated me, Paolo! In America, Paolo, I still have the reputation of being a woman of talent and beauty. Fashion magazines are still eager to have portraits of me endorsing things like cigarettes and cosmetics. Plays have been written for me and books about me. Ask anybody who has ever been to London or New York or Paris, anybody will tell you, even your friend, the Contessa, that I am not a person to be treated like the Signora Coogan was treated. When we get home, Paolo, maybe not tonight, since people are going to be there, but some time tomorrow, I will take out a collection of theatrical souvenirs that my husband kept for me and you will see for yourself and I will not have to tell you!

So it had happened. It had been lost, all dignity, and now she was frantically digging a handkerchief and a compact out of her bag while her breath came in sobs.

The car was turning up the Via Gregoriana.

Forcibly she stopped sobbing and opened the compact.

Paolo was talking.

Yes, I have seen your pictures in the fashion magazines, too. But since you have brought up this subject, which I don't think is a very dignified subject, let me remind you that I have been photographed, too, by Settimana Incom, to mention one instance, and not merely photographed but have had my picture painted by some of the most famous artists of Europe. And you are not the first great lady that I have gone out with. No, but last season, the winter before I met you, I travelled all over

Morocco and Andalusia in the party of Mrs. Jamison Walker who has been photographed by more fashion magazines in one month than most people see in a year!

The car had arrived at the gate to the palazzo.

You are right, Paolo, said Mrs. Stone as they waited for the portière to let them in, it is not a dignified subject, and I think the worst thing about love between a very young and a somewhat older person is the terrifying loss of dignity that it seems to call for . . .

The Contessa and three younger women were already assembled in Mrs. Stone's apartment waiting for her return. One of the guests was a young American film-actress and it was on her account that the evening had been arranged. It was only yesterday that the old lady had decided to repair the misunderstanding between herself and Paolo. She had used the film-actress as a bait, like a lump of sugar to coax a fettlesome pony back into a stable. On the phone she had told Paolo that the young actress was between husbands and unmistakably bored. I am certain there is more to be gained in this quarter, said the Contessa, than you have managed to get out of the Signora Stone, and I am not speaking of anything strictly material. Because you know, Paolo, caro, you are not just another beautiful young man, there is more to you than that, you have a style, you have distinction, you have something that millions of women would respond to on the screen!

This gesture of the Contessa's was related in motive to a disappointment that she had recently suffered in a call that she had paid Mrs. Stone. At that time the Contessa had decided to liquidate her interest in Mrs. Stone's Roman career, and had accordingly approached her for the loan of a thousand dollars. The amount she obtained was considerably less than that. Mrs. Stone had offered the lame excuse that her accounts were tied up by some obscure litigation in the States.

Now while the company was waiting for Mrs. Stone, the Contessa looked into her brandy-glass and saw danger there. Expecting a dinner invitation which had failed to materialize, the old lady had eaten very little that day, and she knew that if she touched the brandy it would go directly from her head to her tongue, but even while she was saying to herself, I mustn't touch it, her rebellious hand was raising the glass to her nostrils, and no sooner had she caught the bouquet than the glass of its own accord, it seemed to her, revolved in her fingers and emptied itself down her throat, which contracted and burned for a delicious instant, and then, an instant later, seemed to turn into the silken thread of a balloon, slipping between two fingers towards the ceiling. As if she stood secretly listening at an outside door, she heard herself speaking the name of Mrs. Stone. It was only the name that she caught very distinctly as she pressed her ear to this

111

mysterious partition, but she caught it over and over again, and she heard the low, excited hum of words stretching between. Now and then she would utter a phrase at which she herself would gasp, though she didn't quite hear it. Nevertheless she felt her lips quivering, all the while, as the drunken wings of an insect above a nourishing flower. As she whispered on, the Roman ladies fluttered greedily towards her, all feeding upon the same intoxicating nectar and the young film-actress fanned their excitement with little suspirations of awe and astonishment. The chairs were drawn close in, for the Contessa spoke in a hushed, rapid tone, darting continual glances at the closed door to the vestibule through which their subject of gossip might be *expected* to enter when she arrived.

But it so happened that Mrs. Stone did not come in by the expected door. She went first to the bedroom to remove her hat and gloves, and Paolo followed her there to brush his hair with cologne. Neither of them spoke nor glanced at the other. They stood before separate mirrors, silent as a pair of thieves, and the electrically thin hum of the Contessa's voice was audible to Mrs. Stone for several minutes before she actually began to listen to it. It was not the Contessa's voice, actually, but an exclamation uttered by the American film-star that first caught Mrs. Stone's attention. The film-star had repeated a certain phrase that was not plain to her, it was the Contessa's brutal clarification of the phrase that had caused the young woman to

112

gasp. At this point Mrs. Stone had moved close to the door but had remained inside it. It is always a disturbing experience to hear yourself discussed by people who do not suspect you are listening. Even when the terms of discussion are quite ordinary, it gives you a curiously unreal feeling. But the terms of discussion that Mrs. Stone overheard were not ordinary and they shocked her to such a degree that all of her recent life was abruptly made visible to her, visible but not intelligible, as if she had been feeling her way blindly along some unknown passage, through absolute darkness, and then, all at once, a flood of light had swept in, and she recoiled in shock and horror from the wall that she had been following with her fingers and from the now suddenly revealed space stretching about her.

Evidently Paolo had also begun to overhear the discussion in the next room, for when Mrs. Stone glanced back at him, his attitude was frozen, cologne and hairbrush suspended on either side of his lustrous head. At her glance he came unfrozen, threw the two articles down and rushed to the door at which she was listening. I don't approve of eavesdropping, he said as he brushed past her and opened the door. He went boldly in. At his entrance, the Contessa uttered a small, startled cry and the others drew guiltily back in their chairs but there was nothing in Paolo's manner to betray that he had heard anything. Mrs. Stone did not follow him immediately into the sala. She watched him being presented to the film-actress, saw him lift her hand towards his lips but drop it unkissed, in the most effete style of Roman gallantry. She saw him repeat the gesture, still more indifferently, with the two younger Roman ladies, and then saw him settle himself gracefully on the arm of the Contessa's chair. And still Mrs. Stone remained on the other side of the slightly open door, neither able to enter nor to retreat from view. They could not have failed to see her standing there with a broad streak of light running down the length of her figure in its shimmering gold dinner gown, but none of them looked towards her. All their eyes kept studiously away from her fantastic state of arrest in the doorway, much as if they were pretending not to have noticed some indecency which had been committed. The Contessa made several stammering efforts to speak. It was evident that an attack of nervous asthma was coming on her again. The others stared at Paolo with the fixed smiles of mannequins, but Paolo had never looked more gracefully reposed. He made no effort to help them out except by providing his example of outrageous ease. One hand fell, as usual, into his lap, and as he spoke casually to the film-star his eyes never quite lifted to hers but played insinuatingly about her mouth and her famous young bosom. And still Mrs. Stone remained standing in the shaft of light through the slightly open doorway, like the audience at a play, so close to the stage that she was bathed in its light. The discomfiture of the Contessa was rapidly increasing. She reached for her brandy glass but she did not seem to have quite strength enough to lift it. When she accomplished that desperate manoeuvre, it was only to discover that the bowl was empty. Then all at once Mrs. Stone heard herself speaking. Paolo, she heard herself saying, the Contessa's glass is weeping! She then found herself moving into the room and going mechanically through the series of greetings and the apologies for having been late. Finally she said to the Contessa, Now, then, you can go on with your story!

By this time the old lady's glass had been replenished and her respiratory disorder was under control, or perhaps it was Paolo's negligent arm on her shoulder that restored her assurance. Oh, she said, I was only telling Miss Thompson about the Signora Coogan's spectacular season at Capri.

That ridiculous old woman! said Paolo. He sprang from the arm of his chair and extended his hand to the film-star. Come outside, he said, and I will show you the seven hills of Rome!

Mrs. Stone was then abandoned to the company of the Roman ladies who began to talk with great animation about the summer opera at the Terme di Caracalla. Mrs. Stone said and heard nothing for several minutes. Meanwhile the butler had set the projector and picture-screen in place. Now he inquired if they wanted to start the pictures. Mrs. Stone signified that they were ready, the lights were turned down, and then with the excuse of summoning Paolo and the film-star, she went out on the terrace. She found it populated only by Paolo and that chilly young moon which had seemed, earlier in the evening, to resemble him so curiously. Where, she asked, is the lady of the silver screen?

Gone, said Paolo.

Why so quickly?

I knew that you would follow us out in less than five minutes, he told her.

I'm afraid that I don't see the connection between that silly remark and my question, said Mrs. Stone.

Her head also felt like a balloon that had escaped from restraining fingers. The liberating influence was not brandy poured over hunger and malice, but the sort of panic that chooses to rush directly into the centre of danger rather than fly away from it.

I told her that you were hysterical, Paolo continued, and I advised her to leave.

This is the third or fourth time tonight that you have insulted me intolerably, cried Mrs. Stone. First at Rosati's when you behaved so outrageously with that drunken girl that I couldn't remain at the table; again, at Alfredo's when you suddenly —

Please, said Paolo, I have a terrible headache!

Your head, said Mrs. Stone, is like that little French clock on the mantel that has a glass case so you can watch all the little wheels and springs working. I know precisely what you are going to say and do just like I know when that clock is about to strike the hour! You are now about to say that you can't stay here tonight. Isn't that so? But it isn't because of a headache, it is because you are going

116

straight from here to the Excelsior to keep an appointment with that cheap little —

Cheap is not a word that you should use, said Paolo.

Don't you think I know why she was brought here tonight? She was brought here because your friend, the Contessa, is a female pimp with a collection of handsome boys she calls marchettas that she disposes of to the highest bidder. But she has found out that I won't engage in that sort of ugly traffic, and so she's decided to pass you along to someone that she thinks will!

I had no idea, said Paolo, that your mind was such a cesspool!

If it's become one it's because of my association with —

Wait! said Paolo.

He clapped a hand over her mouth. The fingers of his other hand dug painfully into the flesh of her shoulder.

Wait, he said, I am going to tell you something. You ought to leave Rome. You ought to leave Rome because you have ruined yourself here and I will not be surprised if the Questura refuses to renew your permesso di soggiorno. Of course that is your business and the Questura's, not mine. But what I personally don't like is your dishonesty!

Paolo, have you gone crazy?

No, I have not gone crazy, and I have not lost my memory either. I remember last February you told me that you were going to help my friend Fabio who lost everything to that rotten priest on the black market!

Oh, Paolo, she cried out.

Oh, Paolo, he mocked.

I thought that was something ugly that I had dreamed, said Mrs. Stone, or if it was real, that now it could be forgotten!

A bad memory is a great convenience, said Paolo.

Paolo, how dare you talk to me like that! she cried out childishly.

Again he pressed his hand to her mouth.

There are people inside that have ears and tongues!

I don't care about people! I demand to know why you have said such awful, insulting things to me!

I said nothing except —

No, you said that —

His fingers pressed so forcibly on her mouth that they stopped her speech altogether for a moment.

You won't listen to me, he hissed. You won't take any warning. You are too puffed up with your glory, your wealth, your magazine fashion-pictures, your wax-paper king of a husband that left you his millions. But this is a very old city. Rome is three thousand years old, and how old are you? Fifty?

Fifty! she gasped.

It was that word that completed her undoing. Dignity she whispered to herself, but it was only the whispering of a word, caught up and swept away in the tempest of her fury.

Paolo had started towards the interior of the

118

apartment, but Mrs. Stone rushed past him with the rapidity of a great-winged bird, and she arrived first at the entrance. She opened the glass doors so violently that the panes shivered and cracked. Afterwards she was not sure what she said to the Roman ladies.

She saw the Contessa's brandy glass slip from her hand but heard no sound as it shattered on the floor. Her own voice she heard but not the words she was crying. The voice itself did not seem to belong to herself, a trick of fancy that she had experienced at moments on the stage, in scenes of violent emotion which she had played so repeatedly that the performance of them was a track along which she moved without thinking. She did not even know that Paolo had come back into the apartment until she felt his hand clapped over her screaming mouth again, nor did she know that she had bit the hand until he tore it away with a shouted curse and struck her in the face with the other.

It should have ended abruptly, all this, but it was grotesquely prolonged by the difficulties of the Contessa in rising to her feet. Her cane slid from under her pressure and she clawed helplessly at the arms of the chair, half rose and then collapsed again. The two other ladies caught her by each elbow and at last got her up, but as they assisted her to the vestibule her legs had the rubbery limpness of a vaudeville comic imitating a drunk.

★ ★ ★

I am drifting, drifting, Mrs. Stone said to herself.

She moved around the apartment. She looked at the very wide white solitude of the bed. She stood very still and listened, so intently that she could hear the clock in the next room ticking. Yes, time was also drifting. And sleep was drifting. Sleep was drifting over the ancient city. If she looked out of the windows, or wandered out upon the terrace, she could see that even the sky was drifting. Everything was drifting. Was there anything else but this enormous drifting of time and existence? Was anything fixed? Oh, yes. That figure of the solitary watcher beneath the Egyptian obelisk. That figure did not appear to be drifting at all. It was still down there in exactly the same position where it had been when Paolo had spoken of it early that evening. But everything else was drifting. Being itself was drifting, and she was drifting. She was drifting again into the front room of the apartment. She had drifted across to the mantel and from it, from underneath the ornamental glass clock which exposed all its workings as it announced the steady drift of time, she removed a piece of magenta stationery folded about two other slips of paper. One was a tiny white card bearing the name of a surgeon in Paris. The other was a small photograph, showing a face of curiously unreal beauty: unreal because it wore no expression, expressionless because the lines of it had been removed by the plastic surgeon whose

120

name was on the card. And on the back of the photograph, in a handwriting that shook with tremors of exultation, was the short message: "This is how I look now!" She looked again at the piece of magenta writing-paper, at the name scrawled at the bottom of it, the name of an old friend of hers. The letter had been on the mantel a long time, yes, since early last winter. Why had she kept it? Was she thinking of *that*? No. No, surely not. But why had she kept the letter, the card and the picture, secretly folded beneath the mantel clock? She put it back there again and she remained standing in front of the mantel watching the shiny brass workings of the clock. A little brass hammer was lifted. It was held poised for a moment. Then three times, in close succession, it struck a tiny glass bell, and then it slipped back into place and made no further movement. But time went on drifting. The continual ticking assured her of that. And she was now drifting again, herself. She had drifted back into her bedroom. Now she was looking again at the very wide white solitude of the bed. It was a landscape of snow, a stretch of pure desolation. Somewhere not visible on its smooth expanse was the wilderness country of sleep in which the night mind drifted without volition among drifting shades that were meaningless or with unknowable meanings. She shook her head, looking at it. She murmured *No* to herself. She would not accept it. And then she drifted into the bathroom and filled a tumbler of water at the tap and came back into the bedroom with the tumbler in her hand, taking little sips of the water without being thirsty. The nothingness continued. The drifting that was nothingness went on. Something, she said to herself. Anything at all, except nothing. Nothing could not be allowed to go on and on and on like this!

A little while later she found herself standing before the balustrade on the terrace.

Now something *was* beginning to happen. It was nothing that she had planned or wanted to happen, and yet she was making it happen. It was happening under her direction, for it was she that had made the sign with the white handkerchief, raised it and lowered it quickly in the night air, and then wrapped in it a pair of heavy iron keys which gave admission to the palazzo. And down there, now, the solitary figure, which alone had not seemed to drift while she was helplessly drifting, had moved from its station beneath the Egyptian obelisk and had stooped to pick up the white parcel on the pavement. It looked up at her, the figure, with a single quick jerk of the head, and even now it was moving out of sight, not away from her but towards her. It was disappearing, no, it had already disappeared beneath the cornice that covered the door to the palazzo, and in a little while now, yes, in a few minutes now, the nothingness would be interrupted, the awful vacancy would be entered by something.

Mrs. Stone looked up at the sky which gave her the impression of having suddenly paused. She smiled to herself, and whispered, *Look! I've stopped the drift!*